I0578343

Daddy Dom 2

Daddy's Naughty Gangster + I Love You, Daddy

A DDLG and ABDL 2 in 1 novel collection of

kinky BDSM age play stories

By Tina Moore

© Copyright 2019 by Tina Moore

All rights reserved.

The content contained within this book may not be reproduced, duplicated, or transmitted without direct written permission from the author or the publisher.

Under no circumstances will any blame or legal responsibility be held against the publisher, or author, for any damages, reparation, or monetary loss due to the information contained within this book, either directly or indirectly.

Legal Notice:

This book is copyright protected. It is only for personal use. You cannot amend, distribute, sell, use, quote or paraphrase any part, or the content within this book, without the consent of the author or publisher.

Table of Contents

Daddy's Naughty Gangster

An ABDL age play romantic story about a college student who finds love with her Daddy Dom and herself as the game changer in his organized crime family

By Tina Moore

Chapter 1

Lucy had graduated top of her class. Her first preference of College had accepted her, and she worked at one of the campus canteens. But like most students, Lucy was broke. After paying for her lodgings, groceries, and phone bill, there wasn't a penny left. She had tried tutoring other students, working extra shifts at work and had even reduced her grocery shopping to a mere $45 a week and yet, at the end of every month, she still came up skint. With the burden of her four-year course still ahead of her, Lucy decided it was time she branched out and got creative.

The following day, she spent the afternoon in her dorm room, searching the internet for different ways she could earn some easy cash. The things she saw made her wonder just how sheltered a life she had really experienced. From finding a website where she could sell her used panties for $50 a pop, to being an adult text chat operator, Lucy had wondered why she had never thought of looking online for jobs before. *Maybe I can get a sugar Daddy or something*; Lucy thought as she created a profile on an interest dating site. She filled in the required sections, uploaded a photo, and waited. Sitting on her bed, she brought her knees to her chest and placed her head on top of her knees. Hearing her phone buzz almost instantly, Lucy frowned in confusion as she saw she had received a message from *DADDY486.*

Hi, I'm Mason, you look cute, little one. I want to see more of you. The message read. Lucy looked at her phone and wondered how she should reply. *It's not like I have to hide the fact I'm looking for his money, the site is called SugarDaddies.com*, Lucy thought as she began to reply.

Thanks, Lucy typed, entirely at a loss for what to write next.

I can see that you are shy, why don't you tell

me a little bit about yourself. I'll go first. I'm 36 and from out of town but have recently moved here for work. I like to keep fit; I'm in the local football team. We aren't very good, just a bunch of guys kicking the ball around really but it's still fun. Maybe you can come and watch sometime. I've got a dog called Huxley, he is a boxer cross mastiff but is a big sook even though he looks scary, Mason replied. Lucy read the message and couldn't believe that she was messaging with this stranger, but smiled as she typed back.

Hey Mason, I'm Lucy. Huxley sounds really sweet. I'm actually studying really close to where you are; I hadn't realized we were so close in location. Have you done this before? Like had a sugar baby? Lucy messaged. She waited for a reply, but when didn't come she messaged the three other men who had contacted her in the time she had been messaging with Mason.

After two hours of constant messaging, she put her phone down. Her head was a frenzy of photos, allowance offers, and sexy messages that had made her wet with desire. Looking up reasons for being ghosted by people online, Lucy took out a box of crackers and read about the troubles sugar babies had experienced and tried to learn as much as she could, just as Mason messaged her back.

Hey, sorry Lucy, I had to quickly get some papers graded that were due back last week. I haven't had to manage my time for a while so I might be a bit rusty at the start as I get back into the swing of making sure you've got everything you need, Mason replied, making Lucy's pussy instantly tingle.

That's ok; I had thought you didn't want to talk anymore, so thanks for the heads up. Do you have time to talk now? Lucy asked back, holding her breath and smiling when Mason answered.

Yeah, little one, how about you tell me the kind of thing you are looking for and I'll answer those questions you asked earlier, Mason replied as Lucy lay back on her bed and began texting him.

Lucy stayed up all night, learning how Mason had

recently got his new job but that he would be transferring departments in the fall. He told her about his past relationships, explaining how some sugar babies and daddies are just scammers, and that he was willing to pay $2000 a week in allowance. Lucy couldn't believe that someone would want to give their hard-earned money away, but she was grateful that Mason seemed to get off on the idea of paying for someone else.

So, like, what do you want from this then? Lucy asked, her eyes growing weary as the time neared midnight.

Well, that's a bit of a loaded question. Now, I just want to let you know right now that if you aren't completely happy to do these things, this won't work out between us ok? Mason wrote making Lucy bite her lip. She nodded her head even though Mason couldn't see her as she saw that he was writing and waited for his response.

I want you to be my submissive. I want a girl who enjoys being teased and tormented before she gets fucked until I am satisfied. And when you aren't my little slut, I want you in diapers. I want to dress you up as a baby and make you drink from a bottle. I want to spank you when you are bad and tie you up so you can't escape from me. I want you to call me, Daddy, and I want you to be my little girl, I want to control the things you wear, the time you go to bed. I want to know the places you go when you aren't in your dorm room, and I want to be able to take you on lavish holidays, Mason explained, making Lucy's eyes grew wide.

You'll send me photos of you wearing the clothes I buy for you and send to you; you'll wear a diaper to bed and send me photo's of that too. We will skype, and you'll show me your pussy before I make you wear a chastity belt under the diaper you'll wear during the day. And if you are a good girl for Daddy, I'll let you cum over webcam, Mason continued, making Lucy freeze. She had never been spoken to like this before; she didn't know how to reply. So she just stared at her phone as the messages came pouring in.

When you aren't my little princess, you'll still

call me Daddy. You'll take my cock whenever I stick it in you without resisting. I can't wait to be sitting on the couch with you, the tip of my cock in your mouth as we watch a movie, your tongue licking it lazily while I play with your tits, was the next message Lucy read, her mouth opening in surprise.

You're going to love my big sack too, my balls are always full, and I can just imagine how you'll feel sitting on my lap with my cock up you and your ass squishing on my big sack, it's like a pillow. But you'll feel that when I make you take one ball in your mouth at a time, Mason messaged. Lucy just read the messages over and over, surprised at how horny she was becoming reading the things Mason wanted to do with her.

Of course, having you fight me a little bit is always hot. But you shouldn't make too much of a fuss, especially when we are in public and I unzip my pants and lock you in place with my hard rod spreading your puffy pussy open. People might see, and Daddy doesn't want to share his little girl. Something else I like to do is tie you to a suspended

X above my bed and spear your cunt with my cock, forcing you to take it as I buck up into you. That's so hot, your pussy will drip onto my cock, and you won't be able to stop me as I plow you. I'll probably have suction cups on your titties too making them sensitive and a gag in your mouth. Yeah, I can just see that now, all bound and open, having to accept where I want to stuff you. Maybe it'll be your ass; perhaps it'll be your pussy, you won't know until I am rubbing your clit and shooting my cum up you, Mason continued, making Lucy wriggle in bed as she read the filth he was sending her.

You like it when Daddy sends you dirty messages, don't you, sweetheart. I bet your pussy is dripping wet; I bet you are trying to stop your juices from wetting your panties. I want you to show Daddy, show me the moist patch on your panties, Mason instructed. Lucy was surprised how her thighs parted at his request as she lowered her phone and lifted up her skirt to take a photo of her light blue panties with the damp patch beginning to show through. Sending it to Mason, Lucy held her breath, hoping that he liked it as she felt her phone vibrate almost instantly.

Oh, Daddy likes, came the message that made Lucy press her panties into her cunt, making them even wetter and sending him a new photo.

You are a dirty girl, aren't you, baby? Mason asked in a new message.

Yes, Daddy, replied Lucy, smoothing her skirt back down over her cum soaked panties.

I don't want this to end, but I guess it needs to so that you can get to sleep, little girl. Tomorrow you'll receive a little reward over that secure money exchange site you mentioned; I'll set up an account on there while you are sleeping tonight. I'm assuming it'll be there by morning. Sweet dreams, little one, Mason said, making Lucy feel a yearning in her heart as his status changed to offline. Looking at the time on her phone, she rolled her eyes. The communal showers would be closed by now; she would have to sleep in her wet panties all night. She thought about changing them but liked that they were dirty because of what Mason had said to her and decided to keep them on. Changing into her short pajama shorts and racerback pink singlet, she traced her nipples under her blankets thinking about what Mason had said, how it would feel to have him suction her titties while he fucked her exposed cunt.

Falling asleep with her phone between her thighs pressing against her cunt, and not feeling the vibrations of her phone making her clit hard through the night, Lucy dreamt of sucking Mason's cock and feeling his generous sack soft against her lips. Waking to her phone vibrating on her clit, Lucy found that she was sucking her thumb as she looked around nervously, hoping that her dorm mate hadn't seen her. Surprised when she looked over to see that she had never come home, Lucy reached between her thighs and rubbed herself before realizing that her phone was still vibrating.

Good morning little baby, Daddy had fun last night, look at the wood you gave me thinking of you this morning, Mason had messaged. Lucy looked at his cock and blushed. *I just want you inside of me now,* Lucy involuntarily replied, her fingers messaging him back before she had realized she had. She looked at his cock and didn't know dicks could look so good. He had pulled back his foreskin, exposing his wet mushroom head that looked like it would need to slither slowly up and down her full pussy lips to spread her open. His thick girth making her suck her bottom lip. He had been right about his sack. Lucy had never seen balls like this before. As his cock lifted up, Lucy saw how his sack was full like he had said, with two clearly defined balls exposed.

Yeah, I'd love to see you choking on this fat knob, running your tongue up and down Daddy's long schlong. You're going to spread those ass cheeks for Daddy's big thumper and take it like the cum dumpster you are, aren't you Lucy? Mason text.

I'm going to bone you till you need Daddy to carry you around campus, so everyone sees that you are my little cock taking princess, he added before Lucy's roommate walked into the room and startled her. Lucy was happy that her roommate was too busy collapsing on her bed after another wild night partying to notice that Lucy's hand had been down her panties, the same dirty pair she had worn all night. Leaving her phone buried in her blankets, Lucy grabbed her toiletry bag and quickly walked to the cupboard, grabbed her clothes, and walked to the bathroom.

Chapter 2

Lucy tried to concentrate on the lecture she had somehow managed to make on-time. The professor was talking about something she had never heard of before, and she knew she needed to pass this class. It was her weakest subject, and although her grades from the other subjects had carried her through the semester, this was the one that would have her passing the semester or not. She had turned her phone off, but as the professor rambled on, all she could think about was Mason and the dirty messages she knew he would be sending her. She had told him she needed to study, and he had told her that it was her problem and not his, that he was going to message her continually all day until she was so desperate to be fucked that she showed him her pussy online that very night.

Don't you dare touch your sluty little cunt baby girl, that's Daddy's now, and I'll tell you when you can touch it. Tonight, pretty baby, tonight you'll show Daddy your pussy. Your Daddy demands it; Mason wrote before she had turned her phone off and hurried into the amphitheater. Lucy wrote down some notes as she thought back to how Mason had said he would deposit her some money on her account as a way of starting their dynamic, and turning her phone back on, Lucy was excited to see if he had done so or not. Trying not to moan at the latest of Mason's messages, Lucy flicked through her phone to see that he had, in fact, sent her $500 with a note attached to the payment.

I hope this finds you well, my darling. It was a far cry from the vulgar messages he had assaulted her phone with, the types that had kept her desperate and horny all day. Looking down to see he had messaged again, Lucy read it before clenching her cunt shut, trying to stop the dripping of cum she could feel escaping her.

I'm going to keep my fat snake filling you as

you bend over in front of me and wiggle your ass for Daddy, once you've been a good girl and done that for me, maybe I'll let you get off your tippy toes, but unlikely. What is more likely is that I turn you around, push you onto your knees and not let you go until you've drunk all Daddy's milk up. Lucy squeezed her knees shut and practically jumped up when the lecture ended racing back to her room and diving under her bed covers as she sighed and rubbed her pussy feverously. *Oh my god, I need to cum, he won't know if I do or not, oh my god, I want him inside of me,* she thought as she began rubbing her clit harder, moaning as she got herself off, happy to finally be alone with her cunt.

"Hi Lucy, nice to finally be able to hear your voice," Mason said three hours later. Lucy had been nervous to see him, worried that she wouldn't find him attractive but as he sat talking to her through her laptop screen, she knew that she had nothing to worry about. In truth, it was her that had started to feel nervous that Mason wouldn't like her. She had dark brown hair that was cut in a trendy style, blue eyes, and an angelic-looking face. Her breasts were one size too big for her body, making her look bustier than she was. Her 5'6 height was fairly average, but her ass had always made her feel self-conscious. The boys at her high school used to call her bootylicious because when she wore sports leggings, her ass would jiggle like a stripper's. She looked at Mason's handsome face, the way he rolled the sleeves up of his button-down business shirt and the gold chain around his neck, growing wet all over again.

"Hey, yeah, it is nice," Lucy replied nervously. Mason liked how she blushed; it turned him on to see her so willing but so timid.

"Did you like the messages I sent you today?" He asked cheekily, a grin forming on the right side of his mouth. Lucy watched as Mason stood up, flexing his hips forward in front of the camera showing off his monster bulge against his handsome business trousers.

"Because I sure enjoyed thinking about you in all those positions and situations," he said. Lucy couldn't see his face; all she could see was his throbbing cock moving under his pants.

"Do you want to say hello to Daddy's big boy, it's important to me that you two are friends," Mason said, pulling on the buckle of his belt with both his hands, pushing his bulge closer to the camera as jiggling it.

"Yes please, Daddy," Lucy found herself saying, the words escaping her lips before she could stop them. Mason chuckled as he pulled open his belt, unbuttoned the top of his trousers and slowly unzipped his pants. Lucy could see the well-fitting grey briefs that housed his thick snake as he pushed through the opening that he had just made and began stroking himself.

"Open your mouth for me, stick your tongue out," Mason instructed, he could still see Lucy although her only vision was of the fat rod he began to pull on. He took his time, shaking his cock in front of the camera before pulling it up as his balls fell out of his briefs.

"This is going to be your new best friend," Mason said, watching as Lucy kept her mouth open and her tongue out, saliva beginning to drip onto her t-shirt.

"I didn't say you could swallow," Mason said as Lucy tried to close her mouth, not used to the feeling of fighting her natural instincts. Mason didn't have to jerk himself for long until he was stiff with the head of his cock, pointing angrily towards the camera.

"He likes you, shake your titties for me," Mason instructed, watching as Lucy obediently shook her huge rack for him.

"Play with them over your shirt," Mason said, smiling as Lucy lifted her hands to her breasts and began groping them. Squeezing them together and following Mason's orders, Lucy leaned back in her chair and put her feet up on her desk, exposing her pussy for him.

"That's a girl. Stroke that pussy for Daddy. I want to fill your dirty little cunt with a nice big load of Daddy cream. You're lucky you're on that side of the computer, or you'd be forced to let me face fuck you hard, like a good girl," Mason said as Lucy stroked her moistening slit.

"Pull your panties off and then get back into that position," Mason said, seeing Lucy disappear only to re-emerge again, this time pushing her skirt between her thighs to hide her pussy from Mason.

"Show Daddy," Mason instructed, his balls filling the palm of his large hand as he jerked his cock with the other.

"Like this, Daddy?" Lucy said, spreading her legs open further and slowly pulling up her skirt. Mason exploded onto the camera the instant he saw Lucy's pussy. Her puffy pink lips looked like velvet, and her glistening hole made him grunt with delight as he gripped his cock hard, wanting to be inside of her. He wiped the camera clean. He sat back down in his chair and shook his head in disbelief.

"And you don't have a boyfriend or anyone

fucking you right now?" he asked, feeling his cock throb.

"No," Lucy said, shaking her head, her titties jiggling as she did so.

"Hey, Daddy," Lucy said confidently, leaning forward and taking her top off. Mason watched as two huge globes popped out from the bottom of Lucy's tight band t-shirt, cupped in a black lace bra.

"Oh, the things I'm going to do to you," Mason said, laughing at how turned on he was.

"Play with your titties. Show me your nipples," Mason instructed, watching as Lucy's pink rosebud nipples emerged from her bra. Lucy licked her fingers and rubbed them over her nipples, making then hard as Mason smiled, thinking of how he would tease them until she was begging him to stop.

"You'll need to wear a bra under your onesie, little girl, I don't want those huge titties to hurt your back," Mason said.

"What's your size?" He added, opening an

internet search, excited to buy her lingerie.

"Um, I actually don't really know, I've never been measured, I kind of just go with what fits," Lucy replied, blushing and looking down, so her hair fell from behind her ear.

"Well. When you feel comfortable meeting up, we can go lingerie shopping and get you fitted properly. I have to look after my little one," Mason said.

"Thank you, Daddy," Lucy replied, lifting her head and tucking her hair behind her ear again.

"Daddy, I think I need to go, my dormmate is meant to be finishing her lecture right now, she'll be home any minute," Lucy said, wanting to dress herself again, worried that she would be found out with her pussy exposed to the computer.

"That's alright, sweetie. Thank you so much for chatting with me this afternoon. You are so beautiful, Lucy. I think we can make each other very happy," Mason said, laughing as Lucy quickly turned the camera off just as he saw the door to her room open.

Chapter 3

Lucy had narrowingly escaped getting caught out by diving into her bed and pretending to be reading a book by the time her dormmate walked into their room.

"Hey," she casually said, as she fell on her own bed and began to flip through a magazine.

"Hi, how was your day?" Lucy said, trying to act normal as her sheets were made wet with the cum that leaked from her cunt onto her soft flannel bed sheets.

"Yeah, it was like whatever. Want to go out tonight?" Ella asked. Lucy had never been invited to a party before, and she blushed not knowing how to act at one.

"Um, I think I'll just stay in, I've got a paper I need to finish," Lucy replied, trying to sound cool.

"Suit yourself," Ella said, flicking her perfect

red hair from one side to the next before standing up and walking back out of the room. Signing in relief for not getting caught out, Lucy quickly got up and locked the door.

"Daddy, I can't wait to meet you in person," Lucy said down the phone the following evening. She had spoken with Mason for the last hour as she sat an off-campus internet lounge and watched as the hipsters typed furiously on their laptops. *I wonder if any of them are actually doing anything important,* Lucy thought.

"It'll be really lovely. We can go for ice cream and walk by the river. We'll go off-campus, so no one gives you questioning looks," Mason replied. With the allowance, Mason had already given Lucy she had a bought new laptop and was looking through his social media accounts as they spoke.

"Did you really win a beer-chugging comp?" Lucy laughed.

"Yes, I have many talents, that is one of

them," Mason said, amused that Lucy was such a curious person.

"Look, baby girl, Daddy, has to go unfortunately but I'll see you tomorrow, alright?" Mason said, causing Lucy to have a knot in her tummy. She didn't want him to go; she wanted to stay with him forever.

"Ok, see you tomorrow, Daddy," Lucy said, smiling as she ended the conversation.

Lucy stayed sitting in the café, watching the people who came in and out. She looked at the way the people interacted and wondered why she never felt like she fit in. *At least with Mason, I feel normal,* she thought deciding to buy a takeaway latte before leaving.

Walking out onto the street, Lucy walked passed the tall buildings with people in fancy suits and the usual mundane city scene. Trains screeching, pigeons searching for crumbs, a deafening noise that reduced everything to silence. *If I lay down here and never moved, no one would even notice,* Lucy thought. She reached into her backpack and took out her earphones, connecting them to her phone and playing a song that seemed to be screaming from her heart. *I wonder what Mason would think if he knew I felt like this. I wonder if he is trying to numb something with this whole sugar Daddy thing as well*, Lucy said to herself sitting on the river bank. She watched the ferries drive past, making ripples in the water, wondering when she would feel something, anything. That was what Mason was for her and she knew it. He was something to explore, a break in the pattern, the pattern that forced itself to play on a loop in her head. The backlash of a hand, the surprise she felt when she learned the world wasn't as she thought it would be. Pulling out a blade of grass, Lucy saw the mountain she needed to climb and wished like hell someone could make the trip for her. *What's the point? When everyone just leaves, will the dream be worth the nightmare? Will it hurt more than the other times, or will somehow this miracle of a man be who I've been searching for,* Lucy asked herself, wanting answers to questions she didn't know how to word.

"Hey baby," Mason said the next day at the spot they had decided to meet. Lucy smiled as he took her hand in his and kissed it before pulling her into his arms.

"You smell yummy," he added, smelling her scent of sweet candy and berries.

"Thanks," Lucy said, nervous and not knowing what to say next.

"Come on, let's go," Mason said kindly. He could see she was nervous and wanted to get her somewhere familiar so she might relax.

"Do you want to hold Daddy's hand?" Mason asked, smiling warmly at Lucy, who just nodded her head.

"Yes, Daddy," Lucy almost whispered. Mason opened his hand to her, and she watched as she placed her hand in his, hoping that she wasn't being a fool and falling for someone who was just going to leave her.

"What is your favorite flavor, baby girl?'

Mason asked as they approached the ice cream store.

"I love choc mint. Which one do you like the best?" Lucy said while Mason held the door open for her.

"Choc fudge twist," he replied, leading her to the chairs at the side of the store. A waitress came over to their table, a waitress Lucy blushed at when she saw her.

"Hey Lucy, cute outfit," Ella said as she eyed Mason. Mason looked at a startled Lucy and rubbed her foot under the table, taking her by surprise.

"Thanks, Ella," Lucy half mumbled as Mason looked at her apologetically. This was the last thing he wanted, to have Lucy closed off and nervous around him.

"We will take two sundaes, one with choc mint and the other choc fudge twist thanks," Mason said, turning back to Lucy, signaling that he was finished with Ella.

"Coming right up," Ella said as she turned

on her heel and happily walked back to the counter to make their order.

"Lucy, are you alright, sweetie?" Mason asked Lucy, who was clearly not alright. Lucy just shook her head and bit her bottom lip.

"That's my roommate," she whispered, looking down and trying to hide her embarrassment.

"Are you embarrassed to be here with me?" Mason asked. Although he was over a decade older than Lucy was, he looked good for his age. With dark brown hair and a handsome face with eyes that could make the naughtiest of girls submit. He had worn tan boots, denim jeans and a white t-shirt, a tan jacket with the sleeves rolled up. He was the type of man who made woman double-take, and who made husbands jealous that his dominance outdid theirs. He had hoped that Lucy wouldn't feel embarrassed about being with him, and he felt intrigued as to why he worried about his appearance with her when he rarely felt self-conscious.

"No, it's not that at all. It's that, what if she finds out that you and I are," Lucy said, trailing off and looking at her sundae Ella put in front of her.

"Thanks," Mason said, smiling politely at Ella.

"I put an extra cherry on yours," Ella whispered in Mason's ear, pretending she was wiping the table down.

"Oh, I don't like cherries," Mason said, annoyed that she was such a flirt. Mason looked at Ella in the eye before raising an eyebrow, dismissing her with a flick of his head

"I thought you told me you liked them?" Lucy questioned, referring to one of their previous conversations.

"I do, but not from her," Mason said, making Lucy laugh and reach out for his hand to hold.
They finished their sundaes as the afternoon sun began to go down, creating a sky of pink and purple.

"Are you ready to go, baby?" Mason asked as he took out his wallet.

"It's ok, Daddy, I can pay," Lucy said which only made Mason laugh.

"Baby girl," Mason said, coming over to sit next to Lucy. He wrapped his arm around her, feeling how she fitted perfectly into his embrace, her breasts pushing into his torso as he held her.

"Daddy also pays," Mason said, kissing Lucy on her forehead. As Mason got up to leave, Ella came over with a milkshake on her tray, picked up their glasses before pretending to slip and pouring the milkshake all over Lucy. Lucy froze, her eyes being to tear up as Mason turned around to see what had happened. Shocked, he walked back, being at Lucy's side in seconds.

"You stupid bitch, look what you have done," Mason growled. He pushed Ella out of the way and went to get napkins, cleaning Lucy and kissing her on her cheek.

"It's ok little one, Daddy will get you some new clothes," Mason whispered into Lucy's ear. Standing up and walking over to Ella, he reached out and ripped the magnetic badge from her outfit.

"You're fired," Mason said, making the girl roll her eyes.

"You're not the manager, you can't fire me," Ella said in a bratty voice.

"No, I'm not the manager, I am the owner, and I don't want sluts like you in my shop," Mason said, before walking out of the store with Lucy following behind him.

"Daddy, do you really own the store?" Lucy asked, excepting the jacket, Mason draped over her shoulders.

"Yes, baby girl. Daddy owns a lot of real estate," Mason said, walking her quickly to a luxury clothing store Lucy would have never even dreamed of going into by herself.

"Daddy, I'm all dirty, I can't go in there," Lucy said, self-conscious and blushing.

"Baby girl, you see this card?" Mason said, opening up his wallet and showing Lucy a black Amex. Lucy raised her eyebrow; she didn't understand what it meant.

"When I leave this card on their counter,

just watch how they spoil you," Mason said, enjoying Lucy's puzzled face. He smirked as he took her hand and led her into the store, ignoring the snobby retail assistants and going straight to the counter. He pulled out his card, put in on the counter like he had told Lucy he would do and eyed the woman with the tight bun, and pulled back smile that looked more like a snarl.

"We are going to need champagne, chocolates and something worth spending money on for this little one. Oh, and close the store, I don't want to be interrupted when I smash your sales goals for the month," Mason said, watching how the woman's eye lit up with the unlimited limit the card held, knowing that her commission would be considerable.

"Right away, Sir," she said, walking swiftly from behind the counter and taking Lucy by her hand. She clicked her fingers at the other woman who quickly locked the doors of the store. The woman led Lucy into a changing room, as Mason sat on one of the large chairs as he waited for his champagne. He looked around the store and sighed a contented sigh while he watched the women dress Lucy in couture. Looking around the store, he got up and went to the belts, wallets, and travel luggage. Seeing nothing that took his interest, he walked back over to where Lucy was changing.

"Maybe we should get you some new lingerie today as well, darling?" Mason suggested, watching as the women scurried off to find her sets of emerald green and deep red.

"Daddy, this is too much. I don't even know when I would wear something like this," Lucy whispered, looking down at the elegant shoes the assistants were buckling to her ankles.

"I guess it's not really college-friendly, is it? How about we get you a few nice outfits, then go somewhere else, somewhere they sell a little more, street style? That way you'll have something for every occasion?" Mason said, dismissing the new heels an assistant was showing Lucy.

"I'd love that, thank you, Daddy," Lucy said,

once the assistants had gone to ring up their purchases. Amongst five pairs of heels, Mason had also bought Lucy three complete outfits, two scarves, four jackets, and two lingerie sets. That had been his favorite, watching as the women had measured Lucy, watching her little face burn red at the touch of another woman. He had also got her two travel bags, a laptop case, keyring, and a phone case. Ringing his assistant to come and collect the items for Lucy, with strict instruction to take them to Mason's house, they paid for the items and left the store. Lucy held Mason's hand as they walked down the street, feeling self-conscious that people were staring at her.

"It's because they want to be you, darling. They wish they could look as beautiful as you," Mason said, kissing the top of Lucy's head and holding her to his side. As they walked from store to store, purchasing boots, sneakers, a new phone for Lucy as well as some gadgets Mason insisted she needed like a camera drone and new wireless earphones, Lucy wondered just how much real estate Mason owned to be able to shop like this.

"Ok, little one, last stop. Makeup and jewelry," Mason said to a tired Lucy. She had never had a day like this in her life, and as the night sky began to fall, Lucy rested her head on Mason's shoulder as the car drove them to the next strip of stores.

"You're very quiet little girl, had Daddy worn you out?" Mason said, loving that Lucy was cuddling into him. She just nodded as she yawned and sleepily looked up at him.

"Yes, Daddy," she said before sucking her thumb. Mason placed his hand on her cheek and stroked her with his thumb affectionately.

"Maybe we should get you home then. Would you like to come to my house and let me get you ready for bed, little girl?" Mason replied, adjusting the headband Lucy now wore. She just nodded her head and closed her eyes again as Mason lifted her onto his lap and cradled her in his loving arms. He smiled down at her, happy that she didn't care about missing out on the final stage of their shopping spree and rocked her gently as their driver drove them home.

Chapter 4

When they arrived at Mason's house, Lucy was already fast asleep. It was near 7:30 pm and the overwhelming day had caught Lucy off guard. As Mason's door was opened for him, he exited the car, Lucy laying like a princess in his arms as his driver smiled at him.

"You have a beautiful girl there, Sir," the older man said. Having been Mason's driver for more than ten years, he had seen many a girl Mason had brought home. He had seen the girl's in the early days, the gold-digging ones who had been brats. He had seen the shy girls, who Mason had introduced to the DDlg lifestyle only to have them run off with another Daddy once they had learned what they liked about the kink. He had even seen the girl who had tried to blackmail Mason, which had almost cost him his fortune. But he had never seen Mason care for a girl the way he seemed to care for Lucy.

"She is something special, Alfred," Mason said, before motioning to the back seat where he had been previously sitting.

"There's something for you and Cherry in the back; I hope she will forgive me for ripping you out of the family BBQ today. I wasn't expecting to need you. Have the next two days off, I have a feeling I'm going to be staying at home this weekend," Mason said. He had bought Alfred a bottle of expensive Champagne and a new watch, the same type Mason himself owned. As for Alfred's wife Cherry, she was always harder to buy for as she thought Mason's luxurious lifestyle was wasteful and was not afraid to let Mason know her feelings. He had loved their jokes, Cherry always complaining Mason didn't do enough for charity and Mason continually reminding her that he gave away millions to charity every year. Today, as a thank you for understanding that Alfred's loyalty was to Mason first and foremost, Mason had bought her a new trench coat, scarf, and sunglasses, knowing that their joke of him one day being able to buy her love would cause her to smirk with satisfaction upon seeing her gifts.

"Oh, Sir. This is too much. Thank you. Cherry won't be able to stay mad at you for very long this time," Alfred laughed, beaming up at Mason. Mason smiled, a tear almost escaping his eye, and Alfred just shook his head.

"No need to say it, Sir," Alfred said, touching Mason's shoulder and nodding goodnight to him. Mason walked up to the front steps of his home, the door opening for him as his butler waited patiently by the door as Mason watched Alfred drive out of the lavish grounds.

"Good evening, Sir, your instructions have been followed accordingly," the butler said as Mason passed him.

"Thank you, have a bath run in the master will you," Mason said, carrying Lucy up the alabaster stairwell and along the hallway to his room. Placing Lucy down on his king-sized bed, he watched as she slowly opened her eyes. Startling slightly, Lucy looked around the room.

"Daddy?" She said in a worried tone, relieved when Mason jumped into bed beside her. Taking off his shirt, Mason enjoyed Lucy reach out for him and touch his defined chest.

"Hey, little lady. You're in Daddy's bedroom. I took you back to my house after you fell asleep in my arms on the car ride," Mason said, lifting her head and putting a pillow under it. Lucy watched as Mason slowly undressed her, biting her lip and not wanting to have sex at that moment.

"Daddy, I think we should wait. I'm not ready," Lucy said, trying to push his hands away. Mason just laughed and took off her headband.

"After everything, I've done for you today, do you really think Daddy is going to start being mean little one? I'm getting you ready for your bed, baby. I'm not going to fuck you just yet," Mason said, picking Lucy up, taking her by surprise.

"Aren't I heavy, Daddy," Lucy asked, feeling

her bottom being rubbed by Mason's large hand as he carried her into his master bathroom.

"No, and even if you were, Daddy isn't going to miss an opportunity to feel all of this," Mason said, shaking Lucy's lingerie covered breasts on his bare chest. He carried her into the bathroom, kicking the double doors open and letting her take in the marble suite before gently placing her in the bathtub. It was warm, just as Mason had expected and watched as Lucy giggled, after being placed in there with her lingerie still on.

"Daddy, you are so silly, now I'm all wet," Lucy said, stretching out in the tub.

"Well, I wasn't sure if you were ready for Daddy to see you're big girl parts in person yet or not," Mason said, taking off his shoes, socks, and pants. He left on his briefs, happy that his semi-hard bulge made Lucy lick her lips involuntarily as he got into the tub with her.

"I'm ready," Lucy said, reaching around her back, wanting to take her bra off. Mason just smirked, reaching for her hands and unclipping the delicate lace garment, before moving his hands over her body and down to her panties.

"Then I guess these are coming off too," Mason said, pulling on her panties. He took Lucy's lingerie and placed it on the steps of the bath before going back to feel her body in his hands. Cupping her tits, he sighed as he felt her nipple piercings, the bars going through her nipples, making them hard and sensitive. Watching as Lucy moved against his touch, Mason felt his cock harden with excitement against briefs. Turning Lucy around, he pulled her into him and continued to play, stroking her soft, plump curves and enjoying their heavy weight. He knew Lucy could feel his cock against her as he pulled her on top of his lap, shuddering as her warm, soft thighs spread on his lap.

"Daddy, you're really big," Lucy said, reaching behind her and placing her hand on Mason's hard shaft. He smiled, reached into his briefs and pulled out his rod, letting Lucy feel it up her back as he reached around and stroked her pussy.

"Pretty shaven girl," Mason said, parting her lips with his finger and searching for her clit. Finding it, he stroked it, pushing Lucy back by her breast with one hand as his other toyed with her clit. Making circles around it, Lucy gasped as Mason pushed her hips forward slightly and repositioned his cock under her and along her slit.

"Sit on it, baby girl, let Daddy have your pussy lips either side of my cock," Mason whispered in her ear. Lucy could feel him pull at her puffy lips, making her sit on him, and her cunt hotdog his cock.

"I thought that would hurt," Lucy said, referring to her sitting on Mason's cock, as he began slowly sliding himself forward and back along her pussy. He just shook his head.

"I like it. I like to feel all of you," he replied, pulling harder on her tits. Lucy just moaned as he played, she had expected that he would simply stick himself inside of her, but this was different. It was sensual, the steam of the bath making the room foggy, the slow but deliberate strokes of his touch making her excited and wet. She had long forgotten that she didn't want to fuck him as he teased her, making her want to say yes to anything he requested.

"Will you let Daddy feel inside of you?" Mason asked, pushing Lucy's breasts together and rolling her nipples in his fingers.

"Yes, Daddy," Lucy said, feeling Mason lift her off him, just to hold her hips above his cock before slowly opening her with his tip.

"Oh, you are a tight little one," Mason said, feeling Lucy's pussy convulse around his head. Trying to enter her, Mason laughed as he was refused.

"You don't want Daddy inside of you just yet, is that it? Or are you just not used to having such a big dick want to explore you?" Mason asked, already knowing the answer.

"I've never had something so big before, Daddy. I do want you, I just don't think I can take you right now," Lucy said, feeling embarrassed she couldn't hold him inside of her. Mason just smirked and pulled out of Lucy, making her gasp as she felt the water around her stretched hole.

"That's ok, Daddy will open you up gently," Mason said, holding her naked body in his arms. Lucy snuggled into his neck, sitting on his lap and feeling his balls under her, his cock along her tummy.

"Don't fall asleep just yet little girl, Daddy still has to dress you for bed, come on, I better get you out of here before you fall asleep again," Mason said, standing up and taking a warm towel from the heated towel rack. He held Lucy's hand as he helped her from the bathtub, admiring her large perky breasts, little waist, and thick booty.

"How did Daddy get so lucky," Mason said as he felt Lucy up while he dried her. Giggling at his groping touch, Lucy wriggled in the towel as Mason dried her.

"Now now, young lady, don't try and get away from Daddy," he said, a slight warning in his voice as Lucy settled and let him explore her.

Satisfied, Mason let the towel drop and took Lucy back into his room.

"Lay down over there," Mason instructed, pointing to a room. Lucy turned to see that he was pointing to a room which had a soft pink light coming from it. Naked, and slightly cold, Lucy walked into the room, shocked at what she saw. *This is what he was talking about,* Lucy said to herself, referring to the requirements of their contract. She remembered how Mason had said he wanted her as his baby girl that she would be diapered, bottle-fed and dressed like a baby.

"I said to lay down," Mason said, gently patting Lucy on her bottom, shaking her soft ass in his hand before pushing her forward. Lucy just remained speechless as she lay down on the changing table that was at the far side of the room.

"Good girl," Mason said, watching as Lucy took in the room. The walls were white with a feature wall of a jungle, with nocks and hooks on the trees to create an animal story. The thick charcoal carpet had a plush white rug in the middle of the room. An adult-sized, white crib was in the corner, and the changing table matched. A built-in cupboard had mirrored doors, and Lucy watched as inside those cupboards housed onesies hung up on wooden coathangers.

"Daddy is going to diaper you every night, little girl," Mason said, taking out a pink diaper and pacifier. Lucy saw that it was glittery and her eye grew big as Mason placed it in her mouth.

"That's a girl," he said, lifting her hips up and placing the diaper under her bottom. Lucy felt the cool powder tickle her as Mason rubbed it over the crease of her thighs meeting her pussy and before she realized it had happened, she was wearing a diaper.

"Don't you just look perfect," Mason said, shaking her breasts in both his hands. Lucy didn't know how to feel as he sat her up and took out one of the bra's he had bought her earlier that day and helped her put it on.

"Daddy will get you some bra's for sleeping in, but tonight you'll wear this," he said, pulling on the straps and admiring his sweet baby girl. He kissed the top of her head as he walked over to the cupboard and looked through the options.

"Hmm, which one," he said, looking back at Lucy who had moved to sit cross-legged on the table. Mason had bought new outfits after seeing Lucy's body on webcam and was happy he had done so. *God her tits are magnificent,* he thought selecting the pink love heart onesie with the deep V at the front to expose Lucy's generous cleavage.

"You are going to look so cute, little one," Mason said as a woman walked into the nursery.

"Will there be anything else for this evening, Sir?" She asked, looking at Lucy affectionately. Lucy just tried to hid her face as she burned red, having someone see her like this.

"No, that's everything, thanks, Ellen. Oh, Ellen, this is Lucy. Lucy, say hi to Ellen," Mason said, making Lucy's head spin.

"Hi, Ellen," she softly said, almost inaudibly. Ellen just smiled as she walked over to Lucy, who Mason was busy dressing.

"It's alright, little girl. I'm the housekeeper here. You'll be seeing a lot of me. And I'll be seeing a lot of you in both big and little girl clothes. So you might as well get used to it, sweetheart," Ellen said. *She is not someone to mess around with;* Lucy thought as Ellen gave her a stern look. She was older than Mason and had the type of motherly figure with wide hips and enlarged breasts. *Probably brought on by hormones,* Lucy said to herself, getting lost in the way they pushed out against her uniform.

"I think she likes you, Ellen," Mason said, seeing how perplexed Lucy was on the older woman's breasts. Ellen just laughed, reaching out to stroke Lucy's soft cheek and hold her head to her breast gently.

"Well, so she should. She'll be on them soon enough," she said, holding Lucy still as she tried to wriggle away, alarmed at what she had just heard.

"That'll be everything, thank you, Ellen," Mason said with a loving smile, dismissing Ellen who kissed Lucy's cheek before dipping her head to Mason and leaving.

"Daddy, what does she mean?!" Lucy said in a frantic hiss, trying to be quiet but only amusing him.

"She runs this household, and she'll also be the one who looks after you when Daddy has to go on work trips or entertain clients during the evening. She's very good; you'll adore her. She's going to spoil you rotten; I can just see it," Mason said, opening one more clip on the front of Lucy's onesie and exposing the tops of her breasts to him. Picking her up and carrying her affectionately, Mason took her to the crib and placed her down gently.

"You're going to sleep here tonight, baby girl," he said, pulling the blankets back and tucking Lucy in. he took a thick fluffy pink blanket from the shelves in the cupboard as well as a selection of stuffies, unsure of which one Lucy would like.

"Daddy, are they all for me?" Lucy said, surprising herself that she fell into this dynamic with so much ease. Mason looked down at the collection he held in his arms as he thought for a moment.

"Yep," he said, deciding that Lucy could have whatever she wanted.

"I like spoiling you, little Lucy, make sure you don't become a little brat, or I'll take all your treats away, alright?" Mason said, dropping the toys on Lucy and making her giggle.

"Daddy!" Lucy said her little voice that she didn't know she had escaping and making Mason's eyes sparkle with affection.

"I won't Daddy; I don't want to make you mad," Lucy said, finding a fat purple kitty that she cuddled into, adjusting all the others around her.

"Goodnight, little one," Mason said, turning on the starry night light that decorated the high ceiling with multi-colored stars.

"Wow," Lucy said from behind her pacifier as her eyes danced across the ceiling, seeing how the stars faded and reappeared in another spot on the ceiling. Closing the door, quietly leaving the room, Mason was delighted how their first meeting had gone.

Chapter 5

Lucy had faded off to sleep, feeling more relaxed than she had in a long time. The yearning for something she couldn't identify ceased to exist in Mason's arms, the pain she carried in her heart seemed to fade away.

Opening her eyes in the morning, Lucy heard Mason before she saw him.

"Yes, that will be fine. The timing is a little off; I have something I need to do here first. But I will be there by tomorrow," Mason said assertively. Lucy guessed he was just outside the closed door and wondered what the day would bring.

"Ellen, call Alfred. I need him tomorrow to take me to the airport. And tell Cherry that it will only take an hour and she will have him back," Mason said as he opened the door to the nursery.

"Well good morning baby girl," Mason said, seeing that Lucy's big eyes with her long eyelashes were staring at him, smiling behind her pacifier.

"Daddy," Lucy said, lifting her arms to hug him as he stood outside her crib.

"Oh, what a sweet baby you are," Mason said, stroking her hair. He unlatched the railing and took down the slat spacing.

"Come to, Daddy, little one," Mason said, carrying Lucy out into the grand living room and placing her on the expensive chestnut leather couch. He set her up with her blankie and kitty before looking at his watch.

"Ellen," Mason called, hearing her quickening heavy footsteps. Lucy watched as Ellen walked into the room, seeing her properly for the first time. She had hazel eyes, lightly tanned skin, and a cheeky smile. Her hair was auburn and set in a fresh blowout with made Lucy wonder how beautiful she looked in her prime if she was this stunning now. *She's got to be like mid-forties,* Lucy thought to herself as Ellen's gaze landed upon her.

"Baby, Daddy has to run into town and pick up the keys to a new property. I was meant to do it Monday, but something has come up, and I need to do it today. Also, I need to go away for a week tomorrow, unfortunately. I know we were going to spend the weekend together, but I now have to be there tomorrow sorry," Mason said, taking both of Lucy's hands in his and looking her in the eye.

"That's ok Daddy," Lucy said, trying not to sound disappointed.

"Good girl," Mason said. Before turning to Ellen.

"Has everything been set up as I asked?" He asked her who just nodded her head.

"Good," Mason said, turning back to Lucy.

"So, I've sorted out that roommate of yours, and you won't be sharing a room with her anymore. I have a feeling she would steal your things, and I can't have my little princess having her things taken," he said, making Lucy look at him curiously.

"Daddy, you didn't, kill her, did you?" Lucy

said, genuinely, making Mason and Ellen laugh.

"No, baby girl. But I did have you moved into your own place. Don't worry. I've paid for it for the rest of the year so you can have your own space. Maybe after this year you come and live with Daddy, but I don't want to rush you. So you've got your own little apartment close to campus and a brand new bike and electric skateboard to get you there," Mason said, making Lucy's head spin.

"Daddy," was all Lucy could see. Seeing that he had made Lucy happy, Mason kissed her on both her cheeks before passing Ellen an envelope and walking out of the room to go and pack his bags.

"So, it'll just be you and me for the day little one. I'll drop you off into your new place in a little while and get you settled in," she said, making Lucy wonder what was in the envelope. Lucy looked up at the woman and wasn't really sure what she was meant to do next.

"Movie and breakfast?" Ellen suggested, laughing when Lucy gave her a toothy smile nodded her head, watching Ellen as she left the room. *What the fuck am I even doing,* Lucy thought, remembering the $15,000 shopping spree Mason had taken her on yesterday without even getting mad when she couldn't take him, how he had been so loving with her and looked after her in the evening.

"Um, Ellen, I have an assignment I really need to get done," Lucy said as Ellen came back into the room with a fruit platter.

"Then you better finish your fruit up little one; Aunty Ellen still has some milky's for you before I let you go," Ellen said, making Lucy's mind spin once again. As Lucy was rendered speechless, Ellen winked at her and fed Lucy a strawberry she willingly accepted.

"Come and cuddle up with Aunty Ellen," Ellen said, opening her arms to Lucy who moved over to cuddle her. Ellen's full breasts feeling like pillows against Lucy's cheek as the movie started. Ellen waited until Lucy's rigid body relaxed and began snuggling into her.

"Oh, you are a sweet little girl aren't you," Ellen said as Lucy sucked on her pacifier, making suckling sounds as she rested her hand on Ellen's breast.

"Sounds like you need a little bit more in your tummy," Ellen said, pulling out Lucy's pacifier and smirking at her pouty face.

"It's alright baby girl, Aunty Ellen will give you something else to put in that little mouth of yours," Ellen said, unbuttoning the front of her uniform and exposing her voluptuous breasts.

"I'm not into girls," Lucy suddenly nervously said.

"I'm not a girl, darling, I'm a woman. And I'm your Aunty so you'll be a good girl for me or you'll feel my punishment on your sweet little ass," Ellen said pulling the front of her bra down and resting her swollen breast on top.

"Don't fight me," Ellen said, putting Lucy into her arms, laying her on her back and rubbing her nipple on Lucy's lips.

"Open your mouth little girl," Ellen said,

slapping Lucy's cheek swiftly as she denied her.

"Don't test me," Ellen said, warning in her voice as Lucy opened her lips.

"There's my good girl. Daddy will be so proud of you," Ellen said, sighing as she felt Lucy's lips tug on her milk filled breast. Suckling, Lucy closed her eyes as Ellen began humming her a tune, relaxing in her arms as Mason re-entered the room, leaning against the wall and smiling at the scene that played out in front of him.

"See you soon, little girl. Aunty Ellen will take care of you while Daddy is away. She's going to check on you every night, alright?" Mason said, holding Lucy's mouth to the older woman's breast when he saw her try to pull away from Ellen.

"Just nod if you understand little one, I don't want to tear you away," Mason said, watching as Lucy nodded her head. He kissed her goodbye and walked out of the room. Ellen continued to hold her as the movie ended and Lucy began playing instead of suckling.

"I think someone is full," Ellen said,

pressing on Lucy's tummy and making her have to fight not to wet her diaper.

"Oh, didn't Daddy tell you, you'll wet your diaper before I let you get back into your big girl clothes," Ellen said to Lucy who just shook her head with Ellen's nipple still in her mouth.

"You can try and fight it. But that will only be painful for you, darling," Ellen said, placing her hand over Lucy's pussy, cupping her firmly. Lucy was surprised at the strength of the woman and wriggled in her arms, making Ellen smirk.

"Last chance," she warned, making Lucy whimper in reluctant obedience. Snuggling closer to Ellen, Lucy buried her face the woman's ample cleavage as she wet her diaper.

"Good girl," Ellen cooed, amused at Lucy's embarrassment. Continuing to hold her, Ellen patted Lucy's padded bottom and turned on the TV.

"I'm going to watch my show before I change you. So you remember to do what I ask you immediately, little one," Ellen said, putting her breast back into her bra and doing the buttons back up. Lucy sat on the couch, hating the feeling of the wet diaper against her skin and whined before Ellen bent her over her knee and gently patted her bottom for the two-hour-long special that played out on the enormous flat screen.

"Come on then. I think you've learned your lesson," Ellen said, rolling Lucy off her lap and watching as she fell on the floor.

"Silly girl, come here," Ellen said as Lucy stood and walked behind her. Ellen led her into another bathroom and gently undressed Lucy.

"Even when you are in your big girl clothes, you'll still call me Aunty Ellen, you do understand?" Ellen said to a nodding Lucy, who now stood naked in front of her. Ellen raised her eyebrow expectantly.

"Yes, Aunty Ellen," Lucy said making Ellen smile and walk away, taking Lucy's clothes and used diaper with her and disappearing as Lucy turned on the shower and let the water run over her body. *What the fuck, Lucy. What is this that you are getting yourself into?* Lucy thought as she let the raindrop feeling water pour down on her head. She had been in such shock by the way Mason had showered her in gifts, the kind of life she had spent years fantasizing over. She looked out of the shower and to her bag that had appeared on the elegant window seat in the bathroom and just smiled as she shook her head. *If all I have to do is fool around with these hot people and get all of this, that's something I can most certainly do,* Lucy decided in the quiet of her heart before turning the water off. Drying off and dressing in one of her new outfits, Lucy left the bathroom with her travel bag over her shoulder. Checking the pockets of the bag, she found her recently bought phone and tablet and smiled at how beautiful and shiny they looked.

"Oh, there you are. Ready to go?" Ellen said, coming out from behind what Lucy could only guess was her room. Why would Mason let the house staff live in his home? Lucy thought, dismissing her curiosity and nodding her head.

She had hardly recognized Ellen as she stood before her in an outfit that made her look as though she was the one who lived the lavish lifestyle. She had that; *I come from generations of extreme wealth*, look about her with her elegance and way she carried herself to match.

"Right, let's go then," Ellen said, her high heels clicking through the house as she led Lucy to the garage.

"We are going in the Porsche, here, give me your bags," Ellen said, taking Lucy's bag off her shoulder and her handbag from her hands. Ellen smirked at how bewildered Lucy was as she looked around at the expensive exotic car collection Mason had acquired over the years.

"Buckle up sweetheart," Ellen said as Lucy sat in the front passenger seat and looked nervous. Quickly snapping into life, Lucy buckled her seatbelt and looked wide-eyed and vulnerable at Ellen.

"Where is my new apartment?" Lucy said in a soft voice, afraid that her life was being taken so far out of her own control.

"It's in one of the buildings Mason owns. It's close to your college; you're going to love it. I put a few of my own touches in as well. We organized it last night while you were asleep. You are lucky to have a Daddy like Mason sweetheart, he is gentle and loving, and there is nothing he can't give you," Ellen said, driving out of the grounds and onto the road. It felt as though Lucy had been living a dream, and within the last 24hours, everything she had ever wanted had become her reality. She looked out the window, letting Ellen's hand fall on her thigh and stroke her affectionately as she drove. Watching the tall trees of the picturesque street turn into the city, Lucy wondered how her new home would look. She was grateful for the first time in years that her real family didn't seem too worried about what she did or didn't do, having been quite blunt in their reaction when she told them she had been accepted into college. They had assumed she would live their life. The life where she had a job at a store and married young, having a few kids who went to the local school and having to find ways to cut costs so they would make ends meat. But that wasn't what she wanted at all. She wanted more; she demanded more. Not from anyone in particular, but from herself. She knew that if she could be college-educated, she would have a better life, and as she saw the building, Ellen was driving her into the garage too, she knew she had been right in some respect.

"Home sweet home, baby girl," Ellen said, parking and getting out of the car. She popped the trunk, got Lucy's bags, and began walking to the elevator, Lucy in tow.

"You'll need these," Ellen said, handing Lucy a key card that she assumed opened the door to the apartment. The elevator chimed and came to a stop, opening its doors and leaving Lucy speechless. There was only one other apartment on this level, and as Ellen opened the door with her own card, Lucy just shook her head in disbelief.

"What, the actual, fuck!?" Lucy said, walking

in circles around the entrance of the penthouse suite.

"Now now, no need for bad language, young lady," Ellen said, causing Lucy to bring her hands over her mouth. She ran to the floor to ceiling, wall-length window and looked out over the city, over the park and lake and could see the flags of her college.

"So, here is everything you need to know about how to operate your new home," Ellen said, showing Lucy a black leather folder on the coffee table.

"And, the fridge and pantry are already stocked. While Mason is away, I will come over every night to get you ready for bed, and every morning to get you ready for your day. Also, I have a card, so does Mason, so if you come home and we are here, don't be surprised. I think that's everything. Oh, one last thing. Everything that you two bought yesterday, is already here, plus a few little treats I got you because I know you didn't have time to buy any jewelry yesterday and well, that simply will not do. You can't be walking around without at least this," Ellen said, taking out a bracelet of diamonds and rose gold and securing it around Lucy's wrist.

"There, perfect," Ellen said, pulling Lucy in and holding her lovingly before kissing her cheek and walking towards the door.

"See you tonight, darling," Ellen said, smirking at Lucy's still shocked expression before closing the front door behind herself.

Lucy just stayed standing where she was and shook her head, trying to understand what had just happened. *He must really like me,* she thought, going to the fridge and seeing that there were fruits and vegetables, dips and meals all labeled with the packaging of expensive restaurants and delis. She took out a bottle of flavored water and sat down on the couch as Mason text her.

Hi sweet girl, I hope everything is to your liking. I've left a timetable for you to fill out on the kitchen bench so I know when it's best to talk with you. Can you fill it in and message it to me? I know you have the assignment you need to get done, finish that today so I can talk to you tonight. Love Daddy x

Lucy got up and walked to the kitchen and looked at the timetable, taking the pen that laid next to it and began filling it out. Sending Mason a photo of her weekly schedule, she wondered if he wanted more. So sending him a photo of her laying on top of the bed in her new bedroom, she wrote.

I can't wait to show you how grateful I am for everything you've done for me, Daddy. Love, your baby girl XX

Mason looked at the photo she had sent and smirked, knowing that she didn't have time to be naughty, he wanted that paper finished.

You're a sweet little tease. But Daddy wants that paper done today. So get busy little girl, I expect perfect grades from you X

Lucy smiled as she put her phone away and went to get her laptop, opening it up and continued to write her essay.

Chapter 6

Mason had been away for the following week just as he had said, with Ellen coming to the apartment every day at 5 pm and staying until 11 pm, just to return at 7 am and stay after Lucy had left for college. Ellen, being true to her word, had regressed Lucy every night, only to trigger her back into being an adult during their mornings together. Mason had video chatted with the both of them every night, enjoying how Ellen mothered Lucy but sending Lucy dirty messages throughout the day until the afternoon.

Yeah, you love it when Daddy sauce squirts into your mouth. Oh, good girl, drink up that protein shake, let Daddy pour it down your throat. It's thick isn't it baby girl. Swallow it all up; Daddy isn't finished with you yet, then you can get your teddy when I am done. You are going to let Daddy take a photo of that cream oozing from your lips, Mason wrote.

Lucy had been sitting in the back row of the lecture theatre so nobody could look over her shoulder at the filthy messages that flooded her phone. Smiling as she wrote back, wanting to match Mason's efforts to make her cum just by reading his texts.

I'd love to feel you cuff my wrists behind my back, Daddy, and make me sit on your lap, your cock spearing my pussy open as your balls slapped against my asshole with each bounce you forced me to take. I'm going to be such a good girl for you and show you my pretty pink pussy, let you fill my tight cunt with your big cock until I have to gasp as it fills me. Mason saw that message as he walked down a corridor and around the corner, breathing deeply as he walked fast as to keep his cock from going hard.

Are you in your lecture now, baby girl? I hope you aren't wearing any panties like you are suppose to. Go sit in the front of the class, spread your thighs and let your lecturer see your pretty pussy. Mason wrote, making Lucy frown. He hadn't said anything about sharing her with another man before, even if her professor wasn't there yet, she knew that within 2 minutes he would be and would have a clear view of Lucy's most private place. Reluctantly, Lucy collected her things and made her way down to the front of the class. Happy that no one ever sat at the front, she spread her thighs, feeling the aircon on her clit and waited for her seedy professor to come in.

Well, aren't you a good girl, Mason messaged next before walking through the glass door of the lecture theatre and looking directly at Lucy who just stared at him with shock. He winked at her, unnoticed by the other students who continued to talk or look through their phones and laptops. Giving a sly smirk, Lucy took her laptop out and pushed her hips forward, giving Mason a better view of her.

"Hello, all you wannabees. how are you

today?" Mason said, making Lucy laugh and the lecture theatre go quiet.

"I say wannabees because up until now you have not had me, and therefore, have been gravely uneducated. But have no fear, Daddy's here now, and I am going to make you great," Mason said making the students laugh.

The lecture continued, with the slutty girls of the course fawning over him and the boys wishing they had the expensive toys Mason had. Lucy's degree was in business and commerce, and the unit Mason was now in charge of was in marketing, or how he liked to call it, 'How to get people to give you their money.' Lucy watched as he dazzled the students for the two-hour lecture, taking more notes than she had ever done in her life. As the lecture came to an end, the students cleared out of the theatre, but Lucy stayed, surprised at how her life was turning out.

"You're Lucy, right?" Mason said playfully as Lucy jumped up from her seat and hugged him tightly.

"I know sweetheart, but we can't do that here. How about I meet you back at yours in about an hour? Daddy wants to see how that little pussy opens up for me," Mason said softly before turning and walking out of the theatre. Lucy walked the other direction, practically ran for her bike and pedaled home as fast as she could.

"Woah, easy there," Ellen said, as Lucy rushed through the front door.

"What? It's only 3 pm, what are you doing here?" Lucy said, surprised to see Ellen. Ellen just raised an eyebrow, swiftly grabbed Lucy by her wrist and pulled her into her, spanking Lucy's bottom quickly and making her double over to try and escape.

"I'm sorry, I'm sorry, Aunty Ellen," Lucy wailed as Ellen belted her bottom with her hand.

"You will be sorry," Ellen said, pulling up Lucy's skirt to see her red handprints on Lucy's skin. Spanking her several more times until Lucy became limp in her arms, Ellen stopped and held

Lucy's chin in her hand, looking at her expectantly.

"I really am sorry, Aunty Ellen," Lucy said. Satisfied as a tear rolled down Lucy's cheek, Ellen let her go and returned to her usual loving self.

"I have put new flowers in the bathroom, and your room, baby girl," Ellen said, as Mason walked through the front door.

"Oh, my favorite girls," he said, copping an eye roll from Ellen who dipped her head to Mason and went to sit on the couch and read a book.

"Daddy!" Lucy said, lifting her arms and jumping into his arms, getting cuddled close as Mason gave her kisses all over her face.

"Ellen, I'm going to go fuck this pretty girl," Mason said, carrying Lucy into her bedroom and kicking the door shut behind him. He walked Lucy over to the bed, kissing her passionately on the mouth, exploring her with his tongue and groaning into her mouth.

"God, you taste sweet," he said, dropping her onto the bed.

"Take your skirt off for Daddy," he

instructed, crossing his arms across his chest and watching her expectantly. Lucy just giggled and got to her knees, reaching around the back of her skirt and slowly unzipping it. Wriggling her hips, Mason loved how the material got caught on her ample booty and reached forward to help her take it off.

"I can't wait to bury my cock in here," he said almost to himself as he reached between her thighs and stroked her slit, licking his lips when he felt how wet she was.

"Yeah, that's what Daddy likes," he said, pulling on her singlet off with his free hand. Lucy just moaned as he toyed with her, rubbing over her clit, and feeling her softness against his rough hand.

"Shake your titties for Daddy," Mason instructed, watching how Lucy's breasts swayed from side to side in her Chanel bra.

"Bounce them," he said, enjoying how they shook.

"Does it hurt, having these big titties shake

for Daddy?" Mason asked, seeing Lucy wince slightly as they dropped with each bounce she did for him.

"A little bit Daddy," Lucy said, feeling Mason push her pussy lips back and slide his finger into her.

"That's ok; you'll learn to love being in pain for Daddy. Just say red like we talked about if it gets too much, but you can take a little pain can't you baby girl," Mason said reaching out and pulling her tits out of her bra and flicking her nipples.

"Such a dirty girl," Mason said as he toyed with her, sticking another finger into her pussy and wiggling his fingers over her G-spot.

"Oh, there is it," he said, watching how Lucy's eyes rolled back and her pussy became wetter.

"Juicy little girl," Mason said, watching as Lucy's hips took over and she began to grind down on his hand. Mason had felt his cock get increasingly hard as he played with Lucy and took her hands to unzip his pants.

"You know what to do," he said, taking her chin in his hand and making her look at him as she felt his cock spring from his pants, his belt buckle hanging from his trousers as she began to give him a handjob with both her hands.

"Can you feel how much I want you?" Mason said, pushing himself into Lucy's hands and letting her chin go.

"Put Daddy in your mouth," Mason said, pushing Lucy's head down onto his waiting rod. Sliding into her throat, Mason was pleasantly surprised how she took him, gagging around his shaft as he filled her mouth.

"Oh, I love that you are just as much of a slut as you said you were. Daddy doesn't like liars," Mason said, pulling out of her pussy slowly as his cock also exited her mouth.

"Lay down," Mason said, positioning himself above her. He slowly stroked his cock, jerking the cum from his shaft and letting it spurt onto Lucy's tummy.

"Let's see," he added, putting the tip of his rock hard cut cock into her.

"Yeah baby girl," Mason said feeling how easily she took him, pushing into her with more intensity and grinning as she gasped for air as his locked his hips down on hers and filled her.

"It feels so good to have you finally," Mason said, keeping his cock inside of Lucy as he kissed her forehead and stroked her hair. He waited until Lucy's muscles relaxed around him, but enjoying how her cunt squeezed him.

"You are a sweet little baby girl, aren't you, Lucy?" Mason said, pulling out of her just to push back in, getting squeezed all over again.

"I'm going to destroy that pretty little cunt," Mason said, holding Lucy's face in both his hands as he began to pound her, kissing her as she moaned. Mason didn't have to wait very long to feel Lucy's cum coat his cock as he pumped her.

"That's it, take Daddy's cock like a good girl," Mason said as he held his hand to her throat and choked her as he came his cum wetting the bed cover as he continued to plow Lucy, groaning as he emptied himself inside of her. Slapping the side of Lucy's thigh as he pulled out of her, Mason looked down at the beautiful girl who willingly gave herself to him and smiled.

"Ellen, come and help my little girl get clean and ready to be my baby girl," Mason yelled, as he bent down to kiss Lucy's forehead before disappearing into the bathroom. Lucy waited for Ellen to come into the room, and she tried to cover herself, which just made Ellen laugh.

"Not much point of that, I've seen your little body all week, haven't I. Did Daddy play his grown-up games with you, baby girl? Are you ready to be little again?" Ellen said, taking Lucy's hand and standing her up, noticing how Lucy doubled forward and held her pelvis.

"Did Daddy hurt you with his big cock? Let's get you in a nice relaxing bath sweet girl," Ellen said, gently reaching around Lucy's smaller body and walking her to the second bathroom and sitting her in the tub. Ellen took the unicorn bubble bath and made the room smell like strawberries as the warm water mixed with the bubbles. She put Lucy's pacifier in her mouth and watched as Lucy didn't try to fight her for the first time all week. Noticing how easily and willingly Lucy regressed, Ellen sat by the bath and tenderly washed Lucy's body with a washcloth.

"We will get you all snuggly, and you can cuddle up with Daddy on the couch, alright?" Ellen said, as Lucy nodded but reached for her.

"You are going to get me wet too, little girl," Ellen said, taking Lucy's arms and putting them back down into the bath. Lucy just pouted, her big wide, innocent eyes softening Ellen's heart.

"Out you come," she finally said, feeling the water turning cold. Lucy noticed how she didn't feel so sensitive anymore and stood still as Ellen dried her, giggling as Mason walked into the room.

"Thanks, Ellen," he said, taking over and putting the towel back on the heated towel rack and taking Lucy's hand, walking her back into her room.

"Daddy, we do it over here," Lucy said from behind her pacifier making Mason laugh.

"Alright sweetie," he said, taking the diaper, Ellen passed him before walking out of the room. Diapering Lucy, Mason dressed her in a pink and black cheater print diaper cover, and black lace Fendi bra, her tight black long sleeve pull-over, over the top.

"Which sockies do you want darling?" Mason said, watching how Lucy crawled over to the cupboard which contained all her baby things. Lucy sat and looked up, trying to decide.

"What do you think?" Mason said, sitting down beside Lucy and making her snuggle into him.

"These ones, Daddy," Lucy said, frowning when Mason shook his head.

"Please, Daddy," he corrected gently.

"Please, Daddy," Lucy said, blushing slightly that she hadn't used her manners. Smiling, Mason stood back up and took down the fluffy pink socks Lucy had selected and rolled them up her cold legs.

"Oh sweetie, let's get you wrapped in a blankie with something yummy and warm to eat," Mason said, walking into the kitchen, followed by Lucy who crawled after him.

"What's for dinner, Ellen?" Mason said, making her raise her head questioningly.

"Well, you're back now, how about you organize it?" She said a smirk on her face.

"Oh, because you just make everything taste so much better than I can. Please, Ellen?" Mason said playfully, picking Lucy up and putting her into Ellen's arms. Holding the young girl to her with loving affection, Ellen rolled her eyes and tenderly reached out to rub Mason's cheek.

"I'm so good to you," Ellen said, kissing Lucy before settling her on the couch with the blankie Mason handed her. Ellen turned on the tv above the roaring fireplace before getting up and walking to the kitchen.

"What would I do without you?" Mason called as Lucy rested her head on his lap. Ellen just mumbled something under her breath as she got dinner ready, enjoying the scene that played out in front of her. Lucy regressed and deep in her little space, Mason watching the football while carelessly patting Lucy until she was almost asleep. Ellen banged a few pots together, waking Lucy up and smirked before going back to cooking.

"Daddy, where did you meet Aunty Ellen?" Lucy said, surprised that Mason's life was nothing like anything she thought could ever exist. Mason just smirked as wondered how to answer her question.

"The same place I met Alfred, the man who drove us around town on our first date," he replied, stopping as Ellen placed dinner on the elegant dining table.

"Up you come," Mason said, picking Lucy up and carrying her to the dining room. Placing her down, she was excited to see her creamy pumpkin soup in her tiger bowl. Her sippy cup next to it filled with a chocolate protein shake and her spoon by Mason's bowl.

"Let Daddy feed you," Mason said as Lucy

reached for the spoon. Lucy felt Ellen drape a pink bib around her neck and clip it up behind her, bending down to kiss her cheek before going to sit down. Mason sipped his beer and sighing as though all the stresses of the day had magically disappeared before taking Lucy's spoon and feeding her, making sure the soup wasn't too hot.

"I'm so happy I could be home for dinner tonight," Mason said, eating his own soup hungrily, receiving more when he had almost finished his bowl.

"Ellen, thank you for looking after my little one while I was away, I hope she wasn't any trouble," Mason said, putting Lucy's paci back in her mouth as she had finished her dinner.

"She was surprisingly good. You got lucky with this little one," Ellen said, getting up to tidy the dishes away. Mason stayed sitting at the table, another beer in his hand as he watched Lucy crawl around the living room floor. She played with her blocks and stuffies, making homes for them and creating stories she then drew about with her crayons.

"I don't think life gets any better than this," Mason said as Ellen came back from putting everything in the dishwasher and turning it on. She had bought a glass of Sherry to the table and sipped it as she too watched Lucy.

"No, I don't think it really does," she said sipping as the fire warmed the room, moving over to the couch and placing a faux fur blanket over her knees as she read her book and Mason listened to an audiobook on real estate buying.

Chapter 7

"Lucy, Daddy's home," Mason called as he entered her apartment. He knew he was early and that she wouldn't be home yet but enjoyed calling out anyway.

"You know she isn't here," Ellen said, surprising Mason when she walked out from Lucy's bedroom after making the bed.

"Oh, what are you doing here?" Mason asked, putting his hands on his hips and looking at her for an explanation.

"I'm working. Your little one can't make a bed to save herself," Ellen said, walking past him and into the kitchen. She turned the kettle on, looking back to Mason who just nodded his head.

"Get me the tea then, it's in the cupboard," Ellen instructed, watching as Mason followed her order.

"Sit down; I need to run through the expenses with you," Ellen said, taking two mugs down from the shelf. She put the tea into the teapot and poured in hot water before placing it on a tray along with the two mugs and carried it over to the table.

"This right here. She's doing it again," Ellen said, opening her laptop and showing him the peak in spending.

"You have to cut her loose. Don't give me your sad sop story about how she needs you; she obviously doesn't. You are just lucky Lucy is so sweet and clueless," Ellen continued

"She's only doing it because she saw me with Lucy on our first date. She's just having a tantrum. This is nothing to worry about," Mason replied, sipping the tea. Ellen just looked at him like he had lost his mind.

"What? She is fun, anyway. She wasn't even meant to be working that day, she must have switched shifts or something," Mason continued, ignoring the looks Ellen gave him.

"We have worked too hard for too long to have that stupid little bitch run us into the ground," Ellen hissed, her eyes now burning holes in Mason. He just sighed an irritated sigh.

"I am aware of how hard we have worked," Mason said, trying to reach for Ellen's hand, only to have her pull away from him.

"Is this because Ella never let you mother her, but Lucy does?" Mason questioned, mischief in his voice. Ellen just rolled her eyes dramatically and scoffed.

"No. It has to do with you bringing a new girl home, regressing her and then leaving her because your spoilt brat called for her Daddy," Ellen said, hurting Mason with her direct manner.

"Ella has been nothing but trouble the minute you showed her the slightest of interests, and I know that thrills you, but Lucy deserves better, and you know it," Ellen said getting up just as Lucy opened the door to the apartment.

"Hi, sweetie," Ellen said, embracing her and kissing her on the cheek.

"Are you going already, Aunty Ellen?" Lucy asked, snuggling into her affectionately. Lucy loved Ellen's sensual smelling perfume and had fallen asleep with it filling her senses on more than one occasion.

"I need to darling; I have some things to take care of," Ellen said, eyeing Mason who just rolled his eyes. Ellen kissed Lucy again before walking out of the apartment and closing the door behind her.

"Don't mind her, she is just a grump," Mason said, coming over and lifting Lucy into his arms.

"Baby girl, how come you never spend Daddy's money or ask if I can get you something else?" Mason asked, catching Lucy off guard.

"What do you mean? You give me my allowance, should I ask for more?" Lucy asked, shocked that he would ask such a question.

"Well, no, I guess not. Why aren't you a brat?" Mason questioned, not understanding why one girl would have a $12,000 shopping spree during her tantrum and the other happy to be given whatever he suited giving her.

"Daddy. I don't understand. Look at everything you have given me! I am so grateful, that's why I'm not a brat," Lucy said, coming to sit next to him. Mason thought deeply as he opened his arms and held Lucy.

"You are the perfect baby, do you know that?" Mason said, taking out his wallet and putting a couple of hundred dollars on the coffee table.

"Tomorrow, go get yourself something nice. You deserve to celebrate," he added, confusing Lucy.

"What am I celebrating?" Lucy questioned.

"The top grade that you got on your paper," Mason said, running his hands over her breasts as he spoke.

"Don't look at me like that. I had your essay cross graded so that no one could ever say it's because you are my sweet and beautiful little one that you got such a grade," Mason said, having his hands slapped away and given a disbelieving look.

"Wow, really," Lucy said, getting lost in her happiness of having succeeded in something she had been working so hard on but not having truly believed she could achieve.

"Yes, so let Daddy have these back, they are like big stress balls. One touch and I'm instantly more relaxed," Mason said, unbuttoning Lucy's blouse and opening it, revealing her ample breasts.

"Oh, is this new?" Mason said, admiring the soft pink lace push-up bra Lucy was wearing.

"Yes, Daddy," Lucy said, reaching around to unclip it. Mason just took her hands away and admired her soft, womanly body. Taking in her form and the gentle creases of her tummy before kissing her passionately.

"Daddy," Lucy giggled, only arousing him further. He lay her down on the couch, loosening his tie and taking off his blue business shirt. Lucy felt his muscled chest and laughed when he wiggled his hips on top of her.

"Lift your skirt up," Mason instructed,

watching as Lucy obeyed.

"Show Daddy," he continued, leaning back off her and looking at her naked pussy. He grinned as she opened her cunt for him and watched as she pulled his rod from his pants, surprised it was already hard.

"Stay like that," Mason said, getting off her and disappearing into the bedroom. Coming back, Lucy saw he carried a tube of lube and a pair of nipple clamps.

"Daddy," Lucy said, resting on her elbows, only to be pushed back down by Mason.

"You don't have to be scared, little one; Daddy wouldn't hurt his baby girl," Mason said, lubing Lucy's pussy before rubbing his wet fingers over his shaft.

"Good girl," Mason said, entering Lucy slowly, feeling her accept him.

"Oh god yeah, baby!" Mason exclaimed hitting her hilt in one slow motion, feeling his balls be squeezed between him and Lucy.

"Oh just let me enjoy this for a minute,"

Mason said a she felt Lucy wiggle, wanting him out of her as she was stretched. Mason kept his cock stuffing Lucy's tight cunt as he pinched her nipples through her bra and clamped the metal objects to her, flicking them and making her pussy relax as her attention went to her breasts.

"That's it," Mason said, pulling out just to push back in it.

"That's sexy," Mason said, placing his hands on either side of Lucy, he pounded her, watching as the clamps shook with each thrust and ragged breath Lucy took. Reaching for Lucy's clit, Mason smirked as he felt her buck her hips, wanting him to give her the release she so desperately craved.

"Not yet," Mason playfully teased as he rubbed her clit faster, wondering how much she could take before she came against his cock. Lucy felt Mason's hands on her wrists as he thrust deeper and harder into her, kissing her as she moaned.

"You can cum now baby," Mason said, not having to repeat himself as Lucy squirted, exciting

Mason who fucked her more vigorously.

"Did you like that baby?" Mason said, pumping her, wanting to shoot his load up her. Lucy just nodded her head as Mason removed his hands from Lucy's wrists and gripped her breasts, shaking them and using them to steady himself as he continued to drill Lucy's wet pussy.

"Daddy's got you," Mason said as he heard Lucy whimper just as he exploded inside her.

"Damn baby," Mason groaned as he felt a shiver go through his body, creaming inside of Lucy again. Pulling out, Mason sat back on the couch and breathed deeply as he closed his eyes and rested his head on the back on the couch.

"Get down here," he instructed, feeling Lucy's mouth on his cock, licking and kissing him.

"Suck it," he said, opening his eyes and looking down, reaching for her tits and laughing as Lucy gagged on his cock.

"My dick looks good in your mouth; I should have had you sucking me off long ago," Mason said, placing his hand on the back of her head and fucking her face until she was gasping for air.

"Swallow that all up baby girl," Mason said, watching as Lucy swallowed the cream he had just pumped into her mouth. Pulling his cock out of her mouth, he laughed as she dribbled her spit and his cum onto the top of her titties, making him reach down and push them together.

"Hold your titties together like that, yeah," Mason said, watching as Lucy shook the clamps as she obeyed him.

"Spit into that deep slit," Mason said, smiling as Lucy followed his orders. Spitting onto his cock, Mason bent his knees as he began titty fucking Lucy.

"Bend your head and stick your tongue out," he ordered, getting his tip licked with each trust forward.

"Oh, you are a good girl for Daddy," Mason groaned, as he came over her tongue, making it slip off her lips and onto her tits. He finished by grabbing the back of her head and cumming over the top of her titties.

"Yeah, you've got those porn star titties baby girl," Mason said, pulling her hands away and enjoying the mess he had made of her.

"Shake those big ol' titties for Daddy," Mason said, watching as Lucy began shaking them from side to side.

"Yeah that's good," Mason said, moving behind Lucy and trying to push his cock back into her pussy, laughing when she took him quickly, bending forward and pushing herself down on him.

"You need a good fuck before you be Daddy's little slut don't you," Mason said, as he began fucking her roughly.

"Yes, Daddy," Lucy moaned as Mason grabbed her hair and pushed her forward, came quickly, laughing and pulling out of her again.

"Let's get you showered," he said, standing back up and watching as Lucy stayed sitting on the floor.

"But Daddy," Lucy said, reaching down to

play with her cunt.

"No baby girl. That's all you're getting tonight. Let Daddy make you his little baby girl now," Mason said, making Lucy roll her eyes and groan in frustration.

"Oh, does someone want to make Daddy mad?" Mason said, laughing at Lucy who quickly jumped to her feet and walked to where Mason was standing. Copping a hard slap on her ass as she passed him and walked into the bathroom.

"Oh, you get started, have a shower. Daddy needs to take this," Mason said, hearing his phone ring. Walking back out to the living room, Mason saw Ella's number on his phone.

"Hi," he said, hearing the water of the shower start, he walked into the laundry and shut the door.

"Daddy, why don't you come over. I need you; I hurt myself," Ella said down the phone, making Mason instantly worried.

"What do you mean you've hurt yourself?" He asked.

"I was getting a drink of water, and the glass slipped from my hands, and I've got cuts everywhere, and there's so much blood," Ella replied, holding her breath.

"Alright, Daddy is on his way. Give me 30 minutes," Mason replied as he ended the conversation. Going back into the bathroom, Mason got into the shower with Lucy who was already clean.

"Baby girl, I have to go," Mason said making Lucy pout but nod her head.

"Work?" Lucy asked. Mason just grimaced and nodded as he quickly washed himself.

"Yeah, baby. Do you want me to get Ellen over here?" Mason said, but Lucy was already shaking her head no.

"I have a few things I need to do anyway," she said, getting a kiss on her forehead and watched as Mason left the bathroom.

Chapter 8

Lucy spent the night looking through social media and eating her weight in junk food. When she had told Mason she had things to do; she had lied. Instead, she had spent the evening tracking him. With all the dirty talk, expensive gifts and learning about a kink she had no idea she loved so much, Mason had never once asked about her. What her dreams were, what her skills were, or even just what she liked. He had no idea she could hack a computer or stick a tracer to his jacket under the collar so he wouldn't find it. He had no understanding that she outsourced her college essays and that he was just one of three other Daddy's who now funded her lifestyle. And with all of the things Mason didn't know about her, the one thing he hadn't learned was that Lucy knew the devil is in the detail. Mason had told her that he was in the real estate business, and yet, when she had gone through his emails and hidden files and checked them against the real estate deals, he had apparently made, his name wasn't on any of it. Ellen's was. So was Alfred's, Cherry's, and a woman named Ella S. But this wasn't the only thing that Mason seemed to avoid having his name on. There were no bank account records in his name. No companies, no shares or stocks. Nothing. Everything was in those four other names. *So, where does all your money come from,* Lucy thought to herself as she began tracking Ellen's accounts.

It was past midnight when Lucy heard her front door open, waking her up and making her realize that she had fallen asleep. Quickly tiding her printed papers and laptop away, Lucy rubbed her eyes as the living room light was turned on.

"Oh my god. I thought you'd be tucked up in bed," Ellen said, holding her hand to her chest, clearly taken aback by Lucy's presence.

"Sorry Aunty Ellen, but Daddy had to work,

so I just stayed up doing my assignment," Lucy said, making Ellen frown.

"What do you mean he had to work?" Ellen said, coming to sit down on the couch next to Lucy.

"We fooled around, had a shower, then he got a phone call and said he had to go to work," Lucy said shrugging her shoulders, somewhat aware that work didn't really mean work. Ellen just angrily sucked in her cheeks before getting up to make a pot of tea. Offering Lucy a mug, Lucy just nodded her head before getting up to put her work in her bedroom. Coming back out into the living room, she sat down next to Ellen and looked her dead in the eye.

"He is seeing someone else isn't he," Lucy asked Ellen who maintained her composure as she tried to think of how to respond.

"No sweetie. He has international clients. So when it's night here, it's the day there. That's why he works such bizarre hours," Ellen replied, reaching out to tuck Lucy's hair behind her ear. Lucy wondered what the relationship between

Mason and the older woman was. She wasn't his mother; Lucy was sure of that. But there was something there. She didn't simply work for him, and she knew Ellen knew exactly were Mason was at that very moment. She also wondered what her role was in the whole thing.

"Let's ring him, shall we? He will be at the office," Ellen suggested, pulling out her phone and finding Mason's number, ringing him before Lucy could form a rebuttal.

"Hi there, Lucy is just wondering when you'll be finished work for the evening. She misses her Daddy," Ellen said, smirking at Lucy who tried to keep up the game she was playing. Ellen nodded her head before speaking again.

"Well, you better finish what you started, because today is a new day and I'd hate to see little Lucy upset for much longer," Ellen said, ending the conversation with a click of her finger.

"He has to stay at the office tonight. Something about tying up some loose ends. He will be all yours by morning," Ellen said, pulling Lucy into her and holding her gently as Lucy fell asleep against her breasts.

Mason had been distant with Lucy for the rest of the week. Sure they had fucked, he regressed her, and they had gone shopping again, but he hadn't been into it. In fact, Lucy was wondering what she could do to excite him and have his attention back on her when it was clearly somewhere else. Ellen had said that it was just because he had been busy at work, but Lucy hadn't seen him at college all week.

"Daddy, how about we do something crazy?" Lucy suggested as they ate breakfast at an expensive restaurant on Saturday morning. Mason looked up from his tablet and raised an eyebrow at her.

"Let's go shooting," Lucy said, making Mason laugh.

"Shooting?" He questioned, receiving a very excited nodding from Lucy.

"We could play dress ups, and you could

teach me how to shoot. There's a range right around the corner from here," Lucy explained gaining Mason's interest for the first time all week.

"Now what makes you think I know how to shoot?" He asked, giving her a curious expression. Lucy just shrugged her shoulders.

"You're good at everything else, I just assume you can do this too," Lucy said honestly. The waitress came to their table to take away their plates, and Mason waited until she was gone before speaking again.

"Well, when you put it that way," he said, his cheeky grin coming back on his handsome face as he got up and helped Lucy from her chair, taking her hand and leaving.

"You have to hold it like this," Mason said coming behind Lucy and doing all the typical boy teaches girl moves. He liked feeling like he was giving Lucy something she hadn't had before and helped her shoot before going to his own rifle and letting off a couple of rounds.

"Woah. This is just what I needed baby girl, thank you," Mason said, lifting up her earmuffs and kissing her cheek. Lucy watched how he emptied the rounds with expert precision. *I thought so,* Lucy thought to herself. She had guessed that Mason had been given some form of formal training and this proved it. He hadn't seen her looking at him as he reloaded without looking at the rifle and began shooting again. *It can't be military; it's something darker,* she thought, coming to stand behind him and wrapping her arms around his waist lovingly. Mason finished the magazine and placed his rifle down, looking down at Lucy and beaming at her.

"You are awesome," he said, holding her affectionately for the first time all week.

"What do you want to do now?" He asked, pouting slightly when Lucy yawned and said she wanted to go back home for a nap.

"You've worn me out, Daddy," Lucy said quietly in his ear. Walking out of the range, Mason and Lucy waited for Alfred to pick them up.

"Do you have to work late tonight, Daddy?" Lucy said, snuggling into him as Alfred pulled up. Opening her door, Mason put Lucy into the back seat as he walked around to jump into the front.

"Riding up here today, Sir?" Alfred asked Mason curiously.

"Yeah, I feel like a change from the back, and Lucy said she was tired so now she can lay down and rest on the way back to her apartment," Mason said. Alfred just nodded as he made a U-turn and began to drive to Lucy's house. Lucy was curious. She took out the recording device from her handbag and placed it in the back of the car, taking the other one out as it had run out of battery. Arriving at her apartment, Lucy got out of the car, kissed Mason goodbye and put her earphones in as the app on her phone activated the recording.

"Sir, we have a problem with the Italians," Lucy heard Alfred say, making her nod her head with the confirmation that something wasn't right about Mason.

"I don't know why. They got what they paid for. If they wanted something extra, that'd have to be another conversation," Mason replied.

"Jimmy, they said they aren't going to wait much longer, you have to meet with the Irish and tell them that they'll have to wait. We need the Italians right now," Alfred said. *Who is Jimmy?* Lucy thought, her eyes going wide when she heard Mason speak again.

"Don't call me that. My name is Mason, Mason Carter. That's who you lot made me. Jimmy is just some street rat who caught a lucky break," Mason said aggressively.

"And don't worry about the Irish. As long as I've got my dick in their pretty little princess Ella, they'll do what I say," Mason said, laughing to himself.

"Also, Ellen wants to know what your plans are with Lucy," Alfred continued, making Lucy interested in his plans for her as well.

"Oh, not you too," Mason groaned.

"Look. Lucy is separate to all of this. She is

beautiful, young, pure. She is the one thing that makes all this shit worthwhile, and I am not getting rid of her just because a couple of gangsters are having an argument. I'll get the guns to the Italians. I'll get the gear to the Irish. And I'll get the cash to the politicians, alright. I haven't let you lot down yet have I?" Mason snarled, making Lucy smile that he thought so highly of her. *So, he's a freelancer;* she thought to herself walking into her apartment, closing the door behind her and leaning against the door. *Ella?* Lucy suddenly thought, wondering if it was the same Ella who she used to share a dorm room.

Chapter 9

"You are awfully quiet today," Mason said as they walked through the park the following week. This had become their favorite spot. Down by the water, the boats sailing in the out on the open sea, people are flying kites up the banks. Here the world seemed simpler. *That's probably why I love it; I don't have to be worried the man I'm sleeping with is the crime lord of the burrow,* Lucy thought as Mason took her hand in his.

"I've just got a lot of work to do. It's almost the end of the semester; there's all there are exams and essays. Honestly, I'm not sure if I can get them done in time," Lucy replied, surprised at how easy it was to talk with Mason. *It's his whole, Daddy, thing he has going on;* she said to herself as he led her to a park bench on top of a hill. The sky was turning a light shade of purple as the sun began to dip down, and Lucy shivered as the park lights came on.

"Are you cold, here," Mason said, taking off his jacket and placing it over Lucy's shoulders.

"Why are you so perfect?" Lucy asked, making Mason laugh.

"Oh, I'm far from perfect. But I can't have my, baby girl, going cold, can I?" He replied. They watched the runners in the park finish their daily exercise before speaking again. Mason had enjoyed the comfortable silence between them. He liked that Lucy didn't feel the need to fill the silence with pointless talking, that she was just happy being in the presence of each other.

"I could just stay here all night," Lucy said, leaning over and resting her head on Mason's shoulder. He moved his arm and held her, bring her closer to his side and kissing her forehead.

"But what about pizza?" He asked in a somber tone, reminding Lucy how they planned to check out a new pizza place which had been given fantastic reviews.

"Ok, I would leave for pizza, but not much else," Lucy said, making Mason laugh as he stood.

"We'd better go, I'm not a fan of parks late at night," he said, holding out his hand to Lucy who excepted quickly.

"What, are you scared?" Lucy playfully asked.

"Yes, actually. And if you knew what happened here after dark, you'd be afraid as well," Mason said in a tone which made Lucy wonder what did go on out here after dark.
The walked the five blocks to the restaurant, Mason being greeted by an Italian man who sat them at the best table which overlooked the city.

"Woah, it is beautiful up here," Lucy said, looking over the city's lights.

"We keep this table reserved for only the best of our customers," the man said, taking the napkin and placing it over her lap. Lucy waited until he had walked away before looking at Mason with a curiosity in her eye that made him concerned.

"How do they know we are good customers?" Lucy asked, her eyes narrowing in on Mason.

"It must just be the beautiful girl I am with. You know what the Italians are like, they know how to appreciate beauty," he replied, sipping his wine and watching fireworks light up the night's sky.

"I don't know how long I will stay teaching at school, Lucy," Mason suddenly said, causing Lucy to whip her head around to look at him.

"What do you mean?" She said, in a pouty voice she used before she could catch it to stop it.

"Well. I think I need to cut back my hours. I thought that I could manage, but it's just a lot right now," Mason said, taking a slice of his pizza and enjoying the cool night's breeze on his face. Lucy ate in silence, thinking of how to gain the information she wanted.

"You mean, between teaching and your other business?" She asked, taking a sip of her wine. Mason just nodded his head. He wasn't going to tell her that he was the man behind the gangs and mob who ran the city. Mason placed his hand on Lucy's thigh and parted her legs slightly.

"You ask a lot of questions my darling, that can be a dangerous thing," he said, the warning in his tone unmistakable. Lucy just nodded and looked down into her lap and bit her tongue. The last thing she wanted was to annoy this obviously powerful man in front of her.

"If you're finished, let's get out of here. I have something special planned," Mason said, taking Lucy's hand and leaving the restaurant. Mason took Lucy's hand and playfully ran up the street with her, jumping on a cable car as it moved up a hill.

"You're exciting," Lucy said puffing and laughing at the same time.

"Well, if you think this is exciting wait till you see the top," Mason said, winking at Lucy and holding her close as the cable car moved into the hills. Passing the homes with the multiple levels and cars Lucy had only seen in magazines, they climbed the steep incline, stopping once they had reached the top.

"Have you ever seen anything as wonderful as the view from up here? It overlooks the whole city, you can see everyone who keeps the pulse of the beast moving and everyone who tries to destroy it," Mason said, coming to stand behind Lucy and wrap his arms over her shoulders. She had to admit; he sure knew how to seduce a girl. They stood there, watching as the city moved below them. The iconic buildings which had always made Lucy feel insignificant now appearing as a mere contribution to the array of lights which dotted the city.

"You know, a house right here would be lovely," Lucy said, making Mason laugh.

"Yeah, and right behind us I would place a huge firepit so that when we would sit out here and watch the world turn, we would have warmth on our backs," he replied, causing Lucy to look at him with her mischievous eyes.

"Hey, I have an idea," she said, pulling away

from him and running towards the forest. Mason followed, worried about what she would find in those dark woods.

"Lucy, be careful," he said with fear in his voice. Lucy hadn't realized he could be scared, and it turned her on to know that she meant so much to him that he would worry.

"Where are you going?" He said, reaching out to grab her hand. She turned into him and kissed his lips suddenly.

"This would be where our bedroom would be," Lucy said, taking off her jacket and placing it on the floor.

"And here, our bed," she said, making Mason laugh and take off his jacket, placing it down next to Lucy's.

"Um, sweetheart, you are on my side of the bed," Mason said, rolling on top of her and making her giggle.

"Oh, here, let me make it up to you," she replied, kissing him again and moaning into his mouth.

"Really? Right here?" Mason said as Lucy pulled her dress up to show him she wasn't wearing panties. She just bit her bottom lip and nodded as Mason excitedly unbuckled his belt and opened his pants.

"Do you want me to help, Daddy?" Lucy said, reaching out to touch his hardening cock. Mason just grabbed both her hands and held them above her head as he jerked himself off, getting hard as he watched Lucy's tits sway with each wriggle she made trying to escape his hand which secured hers.

"Don't make a sound," Mason instructed as he used his other hand to spread her pussy lips and tease her clit.

"Daddy is going to get you wet, little one," Mason said as he watched Lucy try to stay silent as he flicked her sensitive clit over and over until she was bucking her hips, craving for him to be inside of her.

"Now you're ready for Daddy," he said, pushing his cock into her tight cunt and laying his body on top of hers as he forced her to take him.

"You are such a good girl," Mason said, staying on top of her but pulling out slightly just to ram her again, feeling her big soft tits on his chest and her breathing coming out in short sharp gasps each time he filled her. Placing a hand over her mouth, Mason let her hands go and watched how Lucy played with her tits as he fucked her with more aggression than he knew she was ready for.

"Just a little longer, you can do that can't you baby," Mason said more than asked as he fucked her hard, holding both her hips down as he watched her tummy push out by the cock he forced into her over and over. Cumming, Mason sighed in relief, worried that Lucy would end their fun before he had been able to. Staying inside of her as he creamed her hole, Mason smirked as Lucy gasped, shocked that he would fill her with so much cum.

"Daddy, I'm not wearing any panties!" Lucy hissed, worried about the cum that would leak from her cunt. Mason just laughed as he pulled out a pull up from the deep pocket of his jacket.

"Then it's a good thing Daddy is prepared, isn't it," he said, pulling it up her thighs and around her waist.

"No one will even notice, your dress isn't tight around your ass, so you're good to go," Mason said reassuringly. Lucy just gave a sigh and rolled into Mason's arms as they watched the night's sky, Mason doing his pants back up in case someone accidentally came across them.

"Did you think that we would have such a good time? Like, have you had this much fun with other girls?" Lucy asked, kissing Mason's cheek.

"Honestly, no. I'm surprised; you are everything that I was looking for. I actually wanted to talk to you about that. You might hear some shit about me with other girls or whatever, but that's just coz girls can get a bit, crazy, when I break it off with them. So, just know that you are my only baby girl right now and that if you do hear some shit, it's just some old ex trying to stir up shit, ok?" Mason said, smiling at Lucy, who just nodded her head, happy that her Daddy was all hers.

Chapter 10

Lucy walked along the hallway to her lecture room in a hurry. She was late. It had been raining, and the roads were slippery as she rode her bike into college. As she approached the room, Ella stepped out from behind the wall.

"So, you're his new pet, hey?" She bitterly said. Lucy just rolled her eyes and tried to walk around her.

"I don't think so," Ella said, grabbing Lucy's hair and pulling her backward.

"I'm talking to you," Ella said, putting her hands on her hips.

"And I'm late," Lucy said, trying to get past again.

"You know. He said you were different," Ella said, causing Lucy to stop and turn to face her.

"Who are you talking about?" She said,

hoping that this Ella wasn't the one with all the deeds to her name.

"Mason," Ella said, a hint of victory in her voice.

"You're, *Ella*," Lucy almost whispered, putting two and two together. Ella just stood there, wondering what Lucy was thinking.

"Yeah. We used to be mates until you came in and sweep Mason off his feet. Didn't he tell you about me? I had thought it was weird he had brought you into the café I work at. I thought it was to rub it in my face. But you don't know, do you? You have no idea who you are fucking?" Ella said, softening as she saw Lucy didn't understand her role in the whole situation.

"That's what he did with me when we first got together as well. Bought me all the things I had only ever dreamt of, took me to places I had only seen in movies. We even went to Paris in the fall and Milan in the spring. He does that, seduces you with a dream," Ella said, somewhat hoping that she was crushing Lucy.

"So, what changed?" Lucy asked, looking down on the ground.

"What changed? You are what has changed. Before you life was great. Now I've been cut off, and the only person who takes my calls is Ellen, and I fucking hate that bitch," Ella scoffed. Lucy looked up and frowned.

"What's wrong with Ellen?" Lucy asked.

"She's weird as fuck. She wanted to dress me up as a baby and stuff. Fucking weird," Ella said, crossing her arms over her chest. Lucy just snorted, trying to suppress her laugh.

"Yeah, that's really weird," she replied, gaining an approving nod from Ella.

"So, what. You want me to end things with Mason?" Lucy questioned, taking out her phone and dialing his number.

"Yeah, I guess," Ella said, putting her hands on her hips again. Lucy pressed call, hearing Mason's phone go off inside the lecture theatre and the students laugh.

"Daddy, Ella's told me everything, and she

is blocking my way into class. I'll be at home if you want to talk," Lucy said, hanging up the phone and putting it back in her pocket before Mason could reply. Shocked, Ella lunged at Lucy but copping a sucker punch to her stomach as Lucy blocked her.

"Don't fuck with me again," Lucy whispered in Ella's ear as she lay doubled over on the floor before turning around and heading home.

Lucy didn't have to wait long before Mason was calling her phone, but ignoring him, Lucy went for a jog. When she got back, she was surprised to see Mason standing in the living room, Ellen and Alfred on the couch and who she had supposed was Cherry standing by the fireplace.

"Lucy, come and sit down," Ellen said affectionately.

"No, you're all scaring me," Lucy said, trying to back away just to have Mason grab her wrist and fling her onto the couch and into Ellen's waiting arms.

"Now now, there's no need for that," Ellen

said, rocking Lucy loving as she tried to calm her.

"What did Ella tell you?" Mason barked. Lucy hadn't heard him use that voice before, and it scared her. Storming over to her, Mason grabbed her chin in his hands and shook her head.

"What did she say!?" He yelled, getting slapped away by Ellen, who held Lucy as she cried into her ample breasts.

"It's imperative that we know sweetie," Ellen said stroking Lucy's hair down.

"She just said that you are with her too!" Lucy spat back at Mason before burying her face in Ellen's breasts once more. Mason sighed, put his hands on his head before reaching out for Lucy, who just flinched and pulled away from him.

"I don't want a Daddy like you," Lucy said, sucking her thumb and looking out at him with broken-hearted eyes. Mason looked around the room at the others, gauging their approval of what he wanted to tell her next. As he made eye contact with each of the other members of his family, each nodding their head to him, he came over to sit next to Lucy who again, pulled away from him.

"Lucy. I need to explain everything to you," he said, gently resting his hand on her leg.

"But before I do, I have to tell you that, I will have to kill you if you say this to anyone," Mason said making Lucy roll her eyes.

"That what? You run game internationally for the two biggest families in the state? I already know that I've known that for weeks," Lucy said, impressed with herself. Speechless, Mason grew cautious.

"Daddy, I tapped your laptop, phone and um, jacket and car," Lucy said, making he equally as amused as mad.

"Here, let me show you," Lucy said, folding the collar of his jacket down and pulling off a stick on transmitter.

"Are you telling me...that we got hoodwinked by an undergrad college girl?" Ellen said, looking directly at Mason.

"I'm very smart, Aunty Ellen," Lucy said matter of factly.

"Too smart," Mason said, shaking his head.

"I like this front you've got; it works really well. But it's too easy to get in. Your cock got you in this mess. Good thing I'm such a good girl," Lucy said, kissing a still shocked Mason on the cheek.

"It always does," Alfred said, going into the kitchen and pouring himself a scotch.

"So, what now?" Lucy said making everyone turn to look at her.

"What do you mean, what now?" Mason said before shaking his head at her.

"No. Don't even think about it. You aren't getting involved. I'm keeping you exactly how you are. My beautiful college student baby girl," Mason said, causing Lucy to roll her eyes.

"But Daddy," Lucy said, making Cherry laugh. Mason just picked Lucy up in his arms and held her tight, not wanting ever to let her go.

"I'm sorry if I hurt you baby girl. I kind of thought maybe you were with the FBI or CIA or something," Mason said taking her into the bedroom.

"Would an agent of the law do this," Lucy said, pulling on his belt buckle and ripping down his pants as she lay tummy down on the bed.

"No, I don't think so," Mason said, cupping her jaw in his hand and sliding his cock into her mouth, only stopping when her eyes started to water. As Lucy's swallowed around his cock, Mason gasped as he felt Lucy's throat open for the first time and take him deeper, almost making his knees weak. Just as Mason began fucking her face harder, Lucy pulled her head back and giggled.

"Nope, not feeling it, Daddy," she said, making Mason look at her in shock. He watched as Lucy got off the bed, laughing as she ran into the office. Following, Mason stopped when he saw her laying on the desk, her hair hanging down the side of the desk.

"I changed my mind again, I'm ready for you now," Lucy said, making Mason laugh and jump up on the desk, pressing his body down on hers.

"God, you feel so good," he said as he pulled

Lucy's panties to the side, spitting on his cock and pushed it inside of her.

"Yeah, this is what I want," Mason said, fucking her excitedly. He pounded her as her moans filled the room, echoed down the hall, and reached the living room.

"Well, I guess he's welcoming her to the family," Ellen said with a smirk on her face. Alfred and Cherry, both just nodded in acceptance of Mason's decision and got up to leave, turning back to see Ellen. She just sighed as she pulled out her phone.

"No, I get to make the call now, we have to deal with Ella," Ellen said, slightly annoyed that the aftermath of that girl was still something she was sorting out.

"You know that this opens us up to getting attacked by the Irish. Having Paddy's daughter was our guarantee of hassle-free transport," Alfred said plainly.

"Yes. I am wildly aware Alfred," Ellen said snapping at him, shutting him down. Alfred and

Cherry, knowing that their contribution to this meeting was over, left the apartment just as Mason strolled through the living room with a sheet around his waist.

"Oh, modesty is a wasted look on you," Ellen mocked, watching as Mason dropped his towel.

"Better?" He asked, swinging his cock from side to side and coping a narrowed eyed glare from Ellen.

"I'm sending Ella home with enough cash and coke to buy Paddy's forgiveness, hopefully," Ellen said knowing how important it was for Mason to maintain the open ports to move the guns through Irish territory to the Italians.

"Ellen, I would be lost without you," Mason said, coming to kiss her on the cheek but getting his dick slapped instead.

"Don't pretend you don't like it," Ellen said, standing up and walking to find Lucy to get her cleaned up. Ellen had plans to turn her back into the little baby she adored so much. It had been a long time since Ellen had had a baby girl and she wasn't about to let any opportunity to be her Aunty go.

Chapter 11

"Baby girl, where are you?" Ellen called through the apartment, looking for Lucy. Hearing her giggles, Ellen walked into the bedroom and saw Lucy rolling on the bed naked.

"Come on, sweetie, let's get you in the bath for Daddy," Ellen said as Mason ran into the bedroom pretending to be a plane.

"Daddy!" Lucy said making Ellen roll her eyes and walk out of the room.

"So, let's put in, all the toys tonight," Mason said, tipping all the bath toys into the big tub splashing the water over the side of the bath making Lucy laugh.

"Daddy, you are so silly," Lucy giggled splashing around the tub.

"Oh this is nice and warm," Mason said shivering in the tub as his body adjusted to the temperature.

"Daddy, let's play hairdressers," Lucy said, swimming over to him and climbing on his lap, putting his hair in a Mohawk and finishing the look with bubbles on top. Mason laughed, reaching for his phone and snapping silly photos of his new hairstyle.

"Oh yeah baby girl, Daddy looks good!" He laughed, before sinking to the bottom of the tub and coming back up aggressively, splashing more water onto the bathroom floor.

"Lucy?" Mason asked, seeing her playing quietly with a bucket and spade. He watched as she scooped water into the bucket and then pretended to make a cake, mixing the water and bubbles and together.

"How'd I get so lucky," Mason said, sitting back against the far side of the tub and relaxing. He watched for another 20 minutes, getting out when the water turned cold.

"Come on, if we stay in there much longer we'll get sick," Mason said, holding Lucy's hooded bunny towel and smiling as she let him put it on her.

"Cute," he said, taking her back into her bedroom and laying her on the bed. Obediently, Lucy lifted her bottom up and let Mason diaper her, tickling her as he stuck the tabs down. He dressed her in her white teddy bear onesie and carried her back out into the living room, looking around for Ellen, who had left a message on a note on the table.

I've gone to clean up a mess, the note read, Mason smiling as he knew precisely what Ellen was referring to, or rather, who Ellen was referring to.

"Well, I guess it's just you and me for the night baby girl," Mason said, opening the fridge to see what they could eat for dinner.

"What about this risotto?" He asked, looking back to see Lucy nodding her head as she colored. She lay on her tummy, her legs swinging in the air as she decorated a page by the fireplace. Mason smiled; he hadn't felt so relaxed in years.

He wasn't sure what it was, but something about taking care of a girl like this made him feel so important and needed. It wasn't about the power or control for Mason; it was about someone seeing him as excellent and kind when he knew that the things he had done in his life were anything but kind.

"Here you go," Mason said, taking Lucy's pink glitter bowl and filling it with the warmed risotto. He sat next to her and let her climb into his lap before he began feeding her, loving how she rested her head on his shoulder, snuggling as she ate.

"Daddy has to go out on business soon little one. I'll be gone for a week. No, I won't be with Ella. I've already had her taken off the deeds so; you have nothing to worry about. I'll get Ellen to look after you, alright?" Mason explained, Lucy just nodding her head and reaching for her blankie. Mason held her, and he leaned forward and grabbed it, waiting for Lucy to snuggle back into him before continuing to feed her.

"Daddy, can we go shopping online tonight, please? I've seen some really cute things I'd love and since you won't be here next week," Lucy said, looking up at Mason with the cheeky smile he loved so much.

"Oh, are you trying to make Daddy feel bad for leaving you?" Mason playfully teased.

"Well no, but if that's how you feel Daddy," Lucy giggled, wriggling out of his arms.

"Can we make a blankie fort and then lay in it when we look at things?" Lucy asked, getting surprised when Mason flung all the cushions up into the air and began designing the fort.

"No, Daddy. It has to go over here," Lucy said, drawing a picture of how she wanted the fort to look.

After an hour of pillow fights, giggling and playing ghosts with the blankies, Lucy and Mason finally had the fort designed and were laying on the pillow bed they had made, looking up at the stars Lucy had made and cut out, sticking them to the ceiling with tape.

"Ok, here, show Daddy what you would like, baby girl," Mason said, passing Lucy his tablet. She flicked through various sites, adding things to her shopping carts as Mason watched her. She selected a variety of new onesies and socks, pacifiers and stuffies. She looked at Mason who just laughed and took the tablet from her hands and clicked buy now, surprised that Lucy hadn't spent over $2000.

"You are so adorable. I don't mind you spending Daddy's money baby girl," Mason said, before going onto another site and clicking through their stock as Lucy fell asleep on his chest.

When Lucy woke, it was late morning, and as she rolled around the blankie fort, Mason was nowhere to be found. Feeling the pit of her stomach drop, she slowly made her way out of the fort and rubbed her eyes sleepily.

"There she is," Mason said, making Lucy instantly happy and relieved that he hadn't gone yet.

"I thought you'd left Daddy," Lucy said,

coming over to cuddle him.

"No, not yet. But I will have to go after breakfast. Sit down at the table; your waffles are almost ready," Mason instructed. Lucy walked over to the table and sat down by her coloring in book and crayons.

"Daddy, I love you," Lucy said, making Mason drop the waffle he was moving from the hot plate to his plate. Giggling, Lucy just sipped her juice from her sippy cup and watched as Mason tried to get his head around what she had just said.

"You love me?" He asked, almost not believing her. Lucy just nodded her head and smiled.

"Yep. I love you, Daddy," Lucy repeated, making Mason beam with joy and run over to her to kiss her on both her cheeks.

"You have made me so happy," Mason said, returning to the kitchen and putting a new waffle on his plate and walking to the table.

"You should probably feed yourself this morning sweetie, have to get you back into your big girl space, or you'll have a tough time going into town," Mason said, pouring syrup over Lucy's waffle.

"Why do I have to go into town, Daddy?" Lucy asked Mason, who was already halfway through his breakfast.

"I have a few things that I bought you, and I want you to go and get them yourself. I was thinking that it would make you feel special to walk around town carrying all your bags," Mason said, putting his fork down and kissing the top of Lucy's forehead before getting up to put more waffles on his plate. Lucy just looked at Mason, his muscular shoulders, loving eyes, and boyish grin. The way his hair swayed when it was not styled and smiled as she thought about how different he looked when he was the in control Mason in public compared to how he was when he was her Daddy in private.

"Done?" Mason asked, pulling Lucy from her daydream and taking her plate away.

"Yeah, thanks," Lucy said, unzipping her

onesie and stripping right there in the middle of the dining room.

"Well, that didn't take long," Mason laughed, coming back and picking up the clothes and diaper Lucy had left on the floor.

"I'm just going to have a shower, be right back," Lucy said, slapping Mason on the ass playfully as she passed him making him look at her with a smirk on his face.

"How did it go with the Irish?" Mason asked Ellen as Alfred drove him to the airport.

"As good as expected. They want their product, though. They don't understand why they have to wait," Ellen said.

"They have to wait because I fucking told them too. And because we haven't got it yet. Did you tell them I'm personally going to go get it and that they'll have it within the week?" Mason asked, drinking scotch and offering one to Ellen who accepted.

"Yes, of course, I did," Ellen replied, sipping

her drink.

"Good. See, everyone will get Christmas on the same day," Mason said as they arrived at his private jet.

"Give this to Lucy," Mason said, passing Ellen a box which had a pair of earrings.

"Make sure she does her homework and goes to class," Mason said before laughing and getting out of the car.

"This is going to work, isn't it?" Alfred said to Ellen as they watched Mason get onto the plane before driving away.

"It has too; we have all spent too many years working on getting to this point," Ellen said, opening the box and looking at the earrings.

"And Lucy?" Alfred said, watching Ellen from the rear vision mirror.

"She's innocent of all of this, and that is how we are going to keep it," Ellen said assertively, looking directly at Alfred who just nodded and turned back to watch the road.

"Anyway. We made all the mistakes on Ella;

Lucy will not be any trouble," Ellen said, more to herself than to Alfred.

Chapter 12

"Ellen, I think someone is following me," Lucy softly said as she hid in a restaurants bathroom.

"Where are you?" Ellen said, getting up from the couch and snapping her fingers at Alfred.

"At, *Hello Chicki*, I'm in the bathroom," Lucy nervously said. Ellen had been fearful of this. That the Irish would take Lucy as an insurance that they would get their product.

"This is what I need you to do. Go to sit at a table closest to the cash register and wait there for me," Ellen said, running with Alfred to the car and getting in, closing the door as the car sped out of the garage and onto the street.

"I'm scared," Lucy said, making Ellen want to be there already.

"Tell me what the men looked like," Ellen

said, wanting to give Lucy a job, so she didn't feel so useless.

"Well, they were in dark jeans, and both had raggedy looking jackets, and they kept going into all the stores I was going into. One asked me if I was having a good day, but I just smiled at him and nodded my head," Lucy replied.

"Good, so you didn't speak with them?" Ellen clarified as they turned into the street Lucy was on.

"No. I thought maybe they were waiting to see if it was me by my tongue piercing," Lucy said, making Ellen smile.

"Clever girl. Yeah, if they haven't taken you by now, they either are unsure it's you and want that clarification, or they are just trying to warn us that they can get close to us. Either way, I'm here now," Ellen said walking into the restaurant and sitting down at the table where Lucy was and turning to see the two men who were following Lucy walk in and search for her. Getting up, Ellen held Lucy's hand as she walked to the men.

"Tell Paddy, it's on the way and that stalking an innocent civilian won't make the shipment happen any faster," Ellen said in a voice Lucy hadn't heard before. It was hard and angry, and the type of voice Lucy was happy had never been used on her.

"Get in," Ellen said, opening the door for Lucy who quickly scurried into the back seat, happy to be safe.

"Maybe don't go shopping on your own anymore," Ellen suggested, peering into the bags and raising an eyebrow.

"Mason bought me them," Lucy said, feeling her face go red which just amused Ellen.

"Who were those guys?" Lucy asked, looking at Ellen but was surprised when Alfred started speaking.

"They are from the Irish mob. Dangerous, dangerous men. You were right to ring us; they would have waited until you weren't in such a public place and then have taken you, holding you captive until Mason delivers," he said.

"It was good that you weren't going to some club or quiet art gallery. I hate to admit it, but once they have you, they disappear like ghosts. We wouldn't have got you back before we delivered and even then, you'd have been changed," Alfred said, a sadness in his voice.

"How do you know so much about the way they work?" Lucy asked, making Alfred slam on his brakes. He turned around to face Lucy and pulled up his sleeve, revealing a grotesque scar that encircled most of his forearm.

"I used to hunt them down, this is a souvenir from those times," he said before turning back around and continuing to drive, leaving Lucy speechless as she looked out the window for the rest of the ride home. *What did he mean, he used to chase them? What is this life I am getting involved in? Is it worth it? I mean, I only wanted some extra money to get me through college,* Lucy thought as they pulled into the garage of Mason's home.

"I think it's best if you stay with us until Mason gets back," Ellen said, Lucy just nodding her head.

"I know you've got classes you need to go to, do you have a burning desire to go onto campus or would you be interested in doing the degree online?" She continued making Lucy's head spin.

"Um, I guess I could do it online. I mean, the goal was to make a lot of money with the qualifications I got there. But I kinda think that I'm good. In fact, I don't really like the degree anyway," Lucy said, surprising herself as the truth she hadn't truly admitted to herself came to the surface.

"So, what are you going to do?" Ellen asked. Lucy just shook her head.

"I don't know. Let me think about it," she replied, taking her things and walking to Mason's room.

She placed her bags down by his bed and climbed into his side, snuggling into his pillow and smelling his cologne on the sheets. *What are my options?* Lucy thought to herself, closing her eyes and trying to picture her life. She imaged, doing her uni degree online. *But for what?* She thought as she opened her eyes again. She was only going to college because she thought that she needed to to get a high paying job to finance her life. *Could I be apart of the family?* She said to herself, looking down at the gifts she had been given from Mason, his only request that she be his baby when he wanted and his girlfriend when he needed somewhere to stick his cock. *It's not a bad life,* Lucy said to herself, biting her bottom lip and making her decision. *I mean, I could do intel, I'm good at that,* Lucy thought walking out into the garden. She walked through the grounds, enjoying the sculpted bushes and colorful flowers and stopping when she found a table and chair set up by the far end of the property.

"Life was simpler then. Boring, broke, but simpler," Lucy said as she saw Alfred coming to look for her.

"Are you having doubts? If you are, it's better you get out now. Mason will understand. He won't cause you any trouble," he said, sitting down next to Lucy. He had brought a thermos of coffee and poured two cups, handing one to her.

"It's just that, I don't want to be a kept house pet," Lucy said, watching as the man nodded his head.

"The thing is, you wouldn't have to worry about this if you haven't snooped around looking for answers. Your conflict doesn't come from deciding to go to college or not; it comes from deciding if you want to blood in or not. It comes from not being sure what position you will have and how your days will go once you step into this life," Alfred knowingly said. Lucy just looked at him while he spoke.

"That's exactly right. It's also not knowing the rules when I can ask questions, what it all means," Lucy said, wishing she didn't sound so pathetic.

"That will all come with time. I have a feeling; Mason will want you to keep studying. You will study law. These are his wishes if you want to stay. He hopes that you will. You'll study law, own a couple of businesses that will make your life easily justifiable. You can have everything you ever wanted Lucy, all you have to do is, take the call," Alfred said, patting her on the shoulder as he passed her and walked back towards the house. Lucy stayed sitting and drinking the coffee, wondering if she was lucky or not. The family wasn't like what she thought they would be; they weren't like the gangster's in the movies. She took out her phone and ended her relationship with the two other sugar Daddies she had, happy that they were too far away to have ever touched her and looked up at the sky.

"It's about to get real," Lucy said out loud as she looked at the clouds moving overhead. She picked up the thermos and cups, got up from her chair and began to walk back up to the house, just as the sun dipped behind the hills.

Lucy stayed at Mason's house for the rest of the week, dropping out of her degree and enrolling through an online university in Law. Mason had been over the moon when she had told him the night he got back.

"Wow, you would really do that? That's amazing!" He said, jumping up from the table and kissing Lucy full on the mouth. He smelt like the jungle and tasted like dirt, Lucy pulling away and looking at him with a puzzled expression.

"I know, I should have had a shower first, but I was just so hungry for a real meal," Mason said, reaching out to hold her hand.

"How come, you've been so successful?" Lucy asked as Mason finished his burger. He looked at her with a curious expression.

"What do you mean?" He questioned, unsure of her meaning.

"Well, how come you never get caught by the feds. Aren't they always after you?" Lucy asked, eating the last of her nuggets.

"Do you know how, when you go to watch a play, you only see the actors?" Mason started explaining, looking at Lucy and smiling at her sweetly.

"Yeah," Lucy slowly replied, enjoying the metaphor.

"Well, the actors are told where to go, what to dress in, how to speak and even portrayed not by their own hand, but by the people backstage. When a play goes bad, it's the cast who gets blamed; no one even thinks about the people backstage, just the two main characters and the whole play is a hit or miss depending on those two people. It's the same thing here," Mason said, getting up to get the soda he left on the kitchen bench.

"Plus, I'm not tied to anything, and everyone is frazzled once a pattern is broken. Our family breaks the pattern. Instead of having a bunch of tough young thugs, we have three mature aged people and me. And for anyone looking in, it looks like I am a successful real estate investor, and they are the people who look after me. You're my girlfriend, and while all of that is true, who we are backstage is completely different," Mason continued to explain.

"Why doesn't everyone do it like this," Lucy asked, taking a sip of Mason's drink.

"Because of ego. They want to be the King, the big dog. I just want to get rich, so I can disappear when and how I want," Mason said, watching as Lucy nodded her head.

"So, this is what we are going to do. I'm going to sell you the apartment you are living in; you are going to be my girlfriend by day, my baby girl by night. You study law online because you are too busy working at, where would you like to work?" Mason said, stopping and looking at Lucy who just shrugged her shoulders.

"You like fashion, tech, jewelry? You want to own a bar? A club?" Mason said, giving Lucy suggestions.

"Maybe in fashion, that's cool," Lucy said, excited about what the future was going to have in store for her.

"Ok, so we make you your own clothing label. Then you work there, and we live happily ever after," Mason said, finishing off Lucy's fries.

"I had no idea life could be like this, I had no idea everything could be so easy," she exclaimed, shocked that she had been handed her life on a silver platter, and even more shocked that it was so easy.

"Life doesn't have to be hard, that's a choice everyone makes," Mason said, stretching his arms out wide.

"And I don't want to make that choice," he added, opening his palm to Ellen who placed a gun in his hand.

"Excuse me, darling, I need to take out the trash," Mason said, standing up and walking towards the back of the house. Lucy watched as he left, smiled to herself, and began designing what kind of clothes she wanted to sell, surprised that Mason's business didn't scare or unsettle her at all.

Chapter 13

Lucy had been working on her outfit designs for a weeks before Mason sent them overseas to be developed.

"Do you think they will understand the direction I want to take with them," she asked over their breakfast. Mason had taken her to a new café which had opened in their neighboring suburb, and over champagne and strawberries, bagels and waffles, Mason had shown her the emails between him and their production warehouse.

"This is so cool; I can't believe that a mere 8months ago, I was some lost college student with nothing but debt and then you came in and saved me like a princess," Lucy said, appealing to his need to save people. Mason had recently begun growing a beard, and Lucy liked that he was even more sensual and dashing.

"Well, I couldn't have all your potential going to waste could I?" He replied, reaching into his jacket to take out a necklace box.

"Open it," Mason said, sitting back in his chair and gesturing to the waiter to refill his glass. Lucy looked at Mason with playful suspicion and opened the box to see a thread of brilliant-cut diamonds set in rose gold.

"Oh my god," Lucy gushed, surprised that he would buy her such an extravagant gift.

"I was hoping you would wear it to the opening of your shop next month," Mason said, smiling at Lucy and standing up to clasp the diamond collar around her neck.

"It's so beautiful, it would be an honor," Lucy replied, touching her new neckpiece.

"Normally, when there's a community or something, a collaring would take place publically, but, it's just you and me kid. So I was wondering, if you wanted, would you consider wearing it after your opening, as a symbol that you belong to me and that no one can take better care of you than I can?" Mason asked. Lucy hadn't seen him so nervous before. She had read up on collaring ceremonies and smiled lovingly at Mason, her eyes already telling him the answer he wanted.

"I want nothing more than to be yours, Daddy," Lucy said, leaning forward and whispering in his ear, placing her freshly manicured hand on his thigh and kissing his cheek before pulling away from him. Mason had taught Lucy how he liked to be adored and worshipped, how he wanted to be greeted in the morning and how he liked his woman to behave and just like the loyal and obedient girl that Lucy was, she had passed every one of his tests with flying colors.

"Good. In that case, we will have to get you a dress to match this beautiful collar," Mason said, standing and holding his hand out to Lucy.

"Shall we, my dear?" He asked, admiring the way Lucy walked in her 6-inch heels.

"I do believe we shall," Lucy replied, tipping their waitress before walking out, her hand held by Mason who walked in front of her.

They walked down the street, going into one shop after another and coming out disappointed continuously with the range of dresses that were on offer.

"Honestly, how hard is it to make a nice dress?" Mason snarled as they exited the fifth store.

"Daddy, I have an idea," Lucy said, taking his hand and leading him down a back street.

"How do you know about this place?" Mason asked, surprised that they were now deep in Italian territory.

"Hello, darling!" A man exclaimed upon Lucy walking into his store; the man all but bowed to Mason who tried not to laugh at the flamboyant gesture and proceeded to walk through the store.

"I need a dress. It's for my store's opening," Lucy said as Mason sat down on a comfortable chair.

"Certainly," the man said, spinning around the room and collecting a handful of dresses before pushing Lucy into a changing room and waiting outside.

"It means a lot for you to come into my store. I am aware of who you are. I am surprised, this could be seen as taking sides," the man said speaking to Mason.

"It is not taking sides. We will get the entertainment from the Irish; you will dress me. You will both be invited. This will be a civil event, seeing as my store is in both of your territories," Lucy said, making the man's eyes widen.

"I see," he said, turning to face Mason who acted as though it was his idea.

"I am to assume you have spoken to all involved parties?" The man asked, turning back to Lucy.

"I have. Ella, Sophia, Danielle, and Skye are all coming, and I've extended the invite to their fathers," Lucy said, knowing the weight behind the words she spoke. This was a political move. She had become acquaintances with the daughters of the four most powerful families who ran not only the Italian and Irish mobs but the commissions daughter as well as the daughter of the candidate who was running for office. She knew that bringing these families together, under one roof, would put her in the limelight and Mason smiled as he watched her become the lady boss he had thought she could be.

"Well, it would be an honor," the man repeated as Lucy came out in a dress that blew Mason away. Involuntarily standing, Mason saw Lucy as a woman for the first time and cleared his throat.

"I thought so too," Lucy said, smirking and turning away from him to look back in the mirror.

"We will take this one," she said to the man who nodded enthusiastically.

"That is an excellent choice," he said, as Lucy went back into the changing rooms to take the masterpiece of a dress off.

"I didn't know you know those girls," Mason said as they walked back down the alley and out onto the main street.

"I don't really, but watch this," Lucy said, dialing a number on her phone.

"Ella. It's Lucy, don't hang up. There is going to be a new store opening, and I think it could be beneficial to your family. Danielle has already confirmed she will be there; I thought if she were going to be there, it would be more than fitting for you also to attend," Lucy said. *As smooth as butter,* Mason thought, smirking as Ella went quiet on the phone.

"You know family is everything to me, I'll be there, send me the details," Ella said before hanging up the phone.

"Now, to call Skye," Lucy said, sitting on a sidewalk bench and dialing Skye's number.

"How do you have all their contacts?" Mason asked. Lucy just laughed and rolled her eyes.

"I hacked their phones," she said in a matter of fact tone that made Mason wrap his arm around her.

"Skye, Lucy, how are you? Look, I'm not

going to beat around the bush. Some stuff is going down, and your Father will want in. I'm sending you the details to an event, make sure you are both there, I mean if you want to win that is," Lucy said, rolling her eyes as Skye began to stutter.

"Who are you?" Skye asked in an innocent voice Mason remembered Lucy having.

"A friend. A friend who can get you everything you want, including Danielle. You being gay is this town's worst kept secret honey," Lucy said, hearing a soft giggle from the other end of the phone.

"Ok, we'll be there," Skye said, Lucy, sticking her tongue out victoriously.

"She's a lesbian?" Mason asked.

"Yeah, I saw her profile last year. Cute really. Too bad her dad's so homophobic. We can work on that too," Lucy said, ringing Danielle.

"Hey, babe, you want some goss?" Lucy asked.

"Yeah," Danielle replied. Mason just sat back and placed both his hands on the back of his head.

"That cute girl from your summer camp last year is going to be at a store opening next month, here are the details. Oh, I've got my doctor calling me, bye," Lucy said, hanging up quickly.

"She isn't one to chat. I met her a few months ago when I went shopping. We bonded over our hatred of wedges," Lucy said, taking a breath for the first time in minutes.

"Ok, this is the tricky one," she said, finding Sophia's number.

"Sophia, hi," Lucy said. Sophia was the daughter of the commissioner and someone who played it safer than safe. Her one weakness, she needed to be needed.

"Look, I need a favor. I am having a store opening party, and I am anxious that no one will come, can I put you down as a guest, you can bring as many people as you want as long as you are there. Please, Sophia?" Lucy said, her little voice escaping and making Mason laugh.

"Oh my god, yes you can count on me. I'll

defs be there babe," Sophia said, making Lucy raise her eyebrow and look at Mason who just slowly clapped for her.

"Thank you so much. I have to go sorry babe; my doctor is calling me," Lucy said, hanging up the phone and smiling victoriously.

"So, now they are all coming," Lucy said, picking up her bag and standing up.

"Do you think you used the doctor line too much?" Mason asked, making Lucy scoff.

"No, I could have multiple doctors," she replied as they walked to the car Alfred had parked up the street.

"This is the new era, Daddy. Long gone are the days where real mobsters hang out in bars and whack people in alleys. The day is rising on us, and I fully intend on running it. The old guys can play their games, they can run their product and have their illegal operations, but it's through the media, politics and having a finger in every single fucking pie that will make us untouchable," Lucy said, making Mason more proud than he had ever been in her.

"You know. I made the right choice collaring you," he said, waving Alfred away and opening the door for Lucy.

"So, what is your next play?" Mason asked, catching Alfred's attention.

"We need to have a family meeting when we get home," Lucy said winking at Alfred.

"I get the feeling we are about to have a very exciting time," he said, making Lucy and Mason laugh.

"That's one way of putting it," Lucy said, turning to stare out the window as she thought through how to execute the next part of her plan.

Chapter 14

When they arrived at the house, Ellen and Cherry were already sitting on the couch with a pot of tea between them. They had obviously not been there very long by the way the pot was still steaming. These were the things Lucy noticed now. Before she would have just seen the two ladies sitting there, now she noticed that the curtains were drawn back but the room wasn't warm enough for them to have been open very long. The steam from the tea told Lucy that they had only just made it and their clothes, while linen, were not creased enough to have meant they had been there longer than 15 minutes.

"So, the baby has a play," Alfred said, walking into the room.

"Alfred, I'm only a baby at night. Please, credit where it is due," Lucy laughed sitting down and pouring herself a cup of tea.

"So, my store will be opening next month, which is only a week away. And you also know that it is smack bang in the middle of the Irish and Italian territories. We also know that things have been good between everyone for a while, but that they could be better. The Italians just had a raid on one of their warehouses, the Irish have had to go underground for various reasons. We also know that the commissioner wants to come down hard on the docks, and the candidate Williamson is making all sorts of promises about coming down hard on organized crime. These are troubling times," Lucy said, sipping her tea.

"If we wanted to hear a report we could turn on the news," Mason teased, wanting to know Lucy's plan. Lucy just looked at him the way he looked at her before she was about to get a spanking, which made him smirk even more.

"But what you have all taught me, is that no one suspects the break in the pattern," Lucy said, waiting for everyone to catch up with her.

"No one would suspect a bunch of girls going to get their nails done at a store owned by an old woman," Lucy said, looking a Cherry who just narrowed her eyes at being called old but smirking as she saw the magnitude of potential Lucy's plan held.

"No one would suspect friends out on a shopping spree. If we hide in plain sight, giving the commissioner low-level criminals from rivaling or wannabee gangs, everyone wins," Lucy said, finishing her tea and looking around the room.

"I think this could work. Everyone is losing money right now, and our common enemy is us. It's our addiction to the struggle of power when we don't need to struggle at all," Lucy said.

"And your plan is to go through the daughters?" Ellen asked, clearly skeptical about the whole plan.

"Yep. Because everybody knows, a real Daddy never says no to his princess," Lucy said, smiling victoriously.

The evening of the store's opening had finally arrived, and so had Ella, accompanied by her entourage. Danielle had come alone, just her security to back her up. Sophia was busy standing next to her father, and Skye was busy looking at Danielle. Greeting them one by one, Lucy led them into the back room of the store and watched as they took it all in.

"Gangster," Danielle remarked, nodding approvingly at Lucy.

"Ladies, have a seat," Lucy said. The four women sat around a round table in the luxurious entertainment room as a song played on the jukebox.

"So. I've invited you here tonight to first, welcome you into the store. But more pressingly, to talk business," Lucy said, looking around the table and into each women's eyes.

"We have all seen the headlines, and we all know whose fault it is that half our families are now incarcerated," Lucy said, looking directly at Skye.

"You know what, no, I am not about to sit here and heard that it's my fault," Skye said, standing up.

"Sit your ass down," Lucy said in a way that made Skye's knees bend instantly.

"The problem is, they are using an old system to do business. Long gone are the days where trench coats and boats ran the city. We are in an era where it has never been easier to move large imports and exports. To catch bad guys in the act, or to win the hearts of the people," Lucy said.

"So this is what I suggest. You want your dad to win this election, right?" Lucy asked Skye, who nodded her head.

"Then you need something that is going to win the hearts of the people. Nothing wins elections like good marketing. So, we will keep his dirty secrets of going to illegal brothels on the border, and in return, you'll get your Daddy to hire one person from each our three families in prominent positions, I'll send you the list later,"

Lucy said, receiving a nod from Skye.

"I need you to leave the docks to your father and start a new trade route. We are going to be flying private from now on. You are going to sell all your real estate and start buying small, boring looking buildings under low-level associate's names, both of you," Lucy said, looking at Ella and Daniella.

"And you, oh you," Lucy said, looking at Sophia. Sophia knew her role in this would be significant. She also knew that Lucy had dirt on her if she was speaking, so openly in front of her.

"You'll take this. I'll send you details of crimes that your Daddy can organize to stop. He will be the hero this city deserves," Lucy said. Sophia just looked at Lucy before sighing and nodding her head.

"And what do you gain from all of this?" Ella asked. Lucy thought back nine months ago and almost laughed out loud that the dynamics of their relationship had shifted so dramatically.

"This isn't about me. This is about us. We

run this city, not the families and not the cops. Us. I'm so sick and tired of men telling me what my place is, that I need to have a good public presence, that I can't step out of line because it will damage what their objectives are. They raised us to be ruthless, whether that's for good or for bad, that's up to you to decide. But while they were busy telling us how to live our lives, they forgot that made us invisible. And no one can catch a ghost," Lucy said, stirring in the other women a truth they had all long kept hidden.

"Look, guns, drugs, the rest of it, it's always been here, what is different now is that we have a say in how it gets organized," Lucy said, receiving agreement from the four women who sat at the table.

"Let's run this bitch," Sophia said, thinking about the heart attack her Father would have knowing she just got into bed with the enemy, knowing full well that is how he got to where he was.

"I want to be president," Skye said making

the other women laugh.

"Then you'd better stick with us," Danielle replied, winking at her and making her blush.

"You know what this means?" Ella said to Lucy, who just nodded her head.

"We could become the biggest organization that this country has ever seen," Lucy replied, raising her glass to the women who sat in front of her.

"To a new era, to us," Lucy said, the those joining with her in both excitement and quiet intensity. Walking back onto the store floor, they parted ways upon kissing each others cheek.

"All good?" Mason said, coming over to Lucy who was looking through the clothes on the rack.

"Yes, it's going to be perfect," Lucy said before taking Mason's hand.

"But I'm tired, can we go home now, Daddy?" Lucy said, reaching for Mason's arm and cuddling into it. He just smiled before walking her out of the store, the cold night air hitting them like a slap on the face.

"I think it's so funny, you're my little gangster baby girl," Mason laughed as Lucy told him how the evening went.

"Everyone has their secrets. Daddy," Lucy said, reaching into her handbag and pulling out her pacifier.

"Look at you. Diamond collar, sexy dress, the highest heels I have ever seen, and a glittery pink paci. How are you so perfect, Lucy?" Mason said as she kicked off her heels and snuggled into him.

"I don't know, Daddy," Lucy replied from behind her pacifier.
The car pulled into the driveway, and Mason carried Lucy from the car like a princess. She never got tired of this, and dramatically posed in his arms, making him laugh.

"I don't want you to be my baby girl just yet, sweetheart," Mason gently whispered as he pulled Lucy's paci from her mouth.

"Do you want me to be your slutty

girlfriend, Daddy?" Lucy sensually whispered in his ear.

"Yeah. You looked so good tonight; I want to do unspeakable things to you," Mason said, letting her drop out of his arms and onto his bed.

"How do you want me to start?" Lucy said, already knowing the answer. Mason unzipped his trousers and let his cock and balls hang in front of Lucy's mouth before pushing them against her lips, making himself hard as he used her.

"Just like that. Open wide for Daddy," Mason said, sticking his dick in Lucy's mouth, groaning as she sucked him deep, opening herself up to him as he pushed in further.

"God you've become so good, baby girl," Mason said, his eyes closing as he arched his back and lifted his arms above his head as he stretched.

"It was a risky move you made tonight, baby," Mason said as he fucked Lucy's face.

"Yeah, and it's about to be even riskier," Lucy said, taking Mason's cock from her mouth and pushing him backward. He watched as Lucy unzipped her dress, her red lace bra had made Mason excited all night.

"God you are beautiful," He said, taking off his long sleeve shirt and kicking off his shoes, followed by his jeans.

"Come to Daddy," Mason growled playfully as he grabbed Lucy's hips and pulled her open pussy to his cock. He grabbed himself, rubbing his dick up and down her slit, watching how she took him as he entered her.

"You always fuck me to gently," Lucy said, almost complaining.

"Oh, really? Would you like it better if I fucked you like this?" Mason asked as he held Lucy's right leg in the air, opening her up more to him as he began to fuck her forcefully. As he plowed her, he was surprised that he didn't like fucking her this way, frowning and trying to fight off the feeling.

"What's wrong, Daddy?" Lucy asked as Mason pulled his cock from her and sat down on the edge of the bed. Mason just put his head in his hands and exhaled deeply before running his fingers through his hair and turning to look at her.

"You've ruined me. I don't want to hurt you. I don't even want to fuck you roughly. I want to make love to you. Lucy, I love you," Mason said, surprised at himself for the way his heart thumped in his chest.

"The thought of taking you like a street whore just doesn't turn me on anymore. I want to watch as your pleasure builds, how you wrap your arms around my neck and match my breathing with yours. I want to connect with you, not just dump and run in you," Mason explained, making Lucy wonder how she could have ever been so lucky to find a guy like Mason.

"Are you trying to be everything I have ever dreamt of?" Lucy asked, making him laugh.

"I thought you'd hate that. I mean, we did meet online for a particular type of relationship. I don't know, maybe having you as my little girl made me only want to experience a softer side to life," Mason said, making Lucy laugh.

"A Softer side? Daddy, there's a dead rat in our basement," Lucy said, referring to the man who Mason had whacked only hours before.

"Yeah, but that doesn't count, that's different. You know how I feel about rats. But with you, it's like I can finally let my guard down, like I can be the man I would be if I worked a 9-5 and we spent 100% of our time worrying about money, like other types of people do," Mason continued as Lucy came to sit next to him.

"So, what now, Daddy?" Lucy asked, her little voice returning as Mason placed his hand on her back and rubbed her affectionately.

"Well, it's time for bathies of course," Mason said, standing up and pulling Lucy into his arms.

Carrying her to the tub, they did their usual bathtime routine followed by a new tradition that Lucy had suggested where they had hot chocolate together while Mason read her a bedtime story.

"Daddy. What if we did just run away like the princess in the story?" Lucy asked as Mason tucked her into her crib. He just laughed.

"Lucy. We don't do that in this family," he said before kissing her cheeks and shutting the door behind him as he left her room.

Chapter 15

"Everything is turning out just the way you wanted it," Alfred said to Lucy two weeks later. Over the past 14 days, the state had successfully raided five warehouses, collecting a total of 35Billion dollars' worth of cocaine, guns, and military weapons as well as ending two of the significant drug gangs. Lucy had laughed that it had been so easy, wondering if Mason would have been jealous wishing he would have thought about joining forces.

"You just watch house prices soar as this becomes a *safer* burrow," Mason teased, knowing full well that the neighborhood was no safer now that it was before.

"It's a free market for the Irish now," Mason added, hoping Lucy hadn't just made a colossal mistake.

"It's meant to be; it's a lot easier holding onto the leash of one dog than it is three. Now they have no competition; there'll be less violence on the streets. A far safer neighborhood," Lucy replied, sipping her coffee and watching the news.

"Oh look, Skye and Sophia are standing together at her Father's landslide victory. How sweet," Ellen said, walking into the room.

"So, where does that leave us with the Italians?" Mason said, turning to face Lucy and giving her one of his serious looks.

"Next time you see Danielle, look at her right hand, I gave her something to think about when she tried to blackmail me into giving her a bigger cut. Greedy bitch," Lucy said, causing Mason to raise his eyebrows, impressed with his baby girl.

"You know, with everyone getting what they want, they'll get bored soon and turn on each other," Alfred said, the warning in his tone almost making Lucy laugh.

"Yes, and that is why I wanted two families

on either side of us because when one steps out of line, it's three against two either way. We are the deciding factor, and they can't touch us. Not because we are so tough, but because we are the ones running the play. They can try and do that, but they'll lose. Unfortunately, the state always wins. The most we can do is make them look bad and reshuffle the deck, but we all know it is only a matter of time until the whole thing blows up in our faces and what will we do then?" Lucy asked, looking around to see if anyone could see what would be coming next. Smiling, when she was clearly the only one who could see it.

"We control the underworld. We bring in our own people; we claim this state as ours. We get a stronghold in every single faction of this city, and we hold it with an unwavering fist," Lucy said, taking Mason's hand and holding it in hers. Surprised, he smiled and reached for her diamond collar and tenderly unclasped it, taking it off her neck.

"A lioness should never be tamed. You are

wild and free, and I will never try to cage you or tie you to my side. You may come and go as you please, but I have no need to collar you," he said, his eyes going wide when Lucy took the collar and put it back on.

"I choose to be yours. You could never collar me if I didn't want you to anyway, let's not get ahead of ourselves. But I love you, and I love what we are building," Lucy said before standing on her tippy toes and kissing Mason full on the lips.

"But how is this going to fit in with your lecturing at the college. Maybe you should sit this one out and just focus on your work?" Lucy playfully suggested making Mason laugh.

"I have already given them my notice. I'm going to open a photography shop, I think it's more me," Mason replied, nodding as he agreed with himself.

I Love You, Daddy

A DDLG and ABDL romantic love story of a tortured woman who finds peace with the love only a Daddy Dom can provide

By Tine Moore

Chapter 1

"I can save you," he had lovingly said. His blue eyes, and toothy smile begging to be needed, as desperate to be loved as she was. Nadia remembered how she had slowly pulled his blue blazer off and unbuttoned his crisp white shirt revealing his chiseled chest — running her fingers over the curves of his pecks, a shiver running down her spine, giving her arms goosebumps.

"No, you can't," she replied in a whisper, her green eyes wishing that he didn't look at her like she was faultless when all she knew to be true was that she was nothing and worthless.

"Isn't that what you want? I know that if you give me a chance, we would be great together. You don't really think that I'm like those other guys do you?" He had persisted. Nadia had reached up and pushed him away at that point, needing distance as he crept dangerously close to the place she kept her pain.

"Don't. Please, I can't," she said, looking at him, wishing she could trust him but not knowing how.

"So that's it? It's over?" He had angrily asked wanting more of her than she was ready to give him, buttoning his shirt back up. Nadia looked at him through tear glazed eyes wishing that she could be the person he thought she was.

"Call it what you want, I'm not who you think I am," Nadia said, pushing past him and crying as she left the changing room of her workplace.

Nadia had seen him several times after that encounter, each time he tried to get too close to her, she would push him away. Unable to tell him what she truly desired, unable to tell him how she knew she liked what she liked. Always running away from him and anyone else who dared get too close to her. Like a damaged pound pup who would cower in the corner of the cage until being scared didn't work anymore. Baring her teeth and letting out an angry snarl before bolting from the confined space she found herself in, Nadia was always on high alert.

Nadia looked at her reflection in the public bathroom mirror at the department store where she worked. Working for a luxury brand in the city had it's perks, sharing a bathroom with the public was not one of them. As she read the back door advertising for what seemed like the hundredth time, she shook her head knowing that somehow this life was not the one she would always have to live.

A storm which had been raging for days had brought the city to a standstill, and the floors were wet and slippery as Nadia slowly made her way out of the store and towards the front door. She was flexing off work early to miss the swarm of people she knew would be all fighting for a seat on the limited buses which waited just outside the store. True to her prediction, the buses lined up as the bells from the cathedral echoed over the city square, signaling the 5 o'clock finish. As people poured from the buildings which blocked the sky, she looked out from the glass elevator and saw the crowds below. People pushing, cutting in front of each other and grumbling at the long wait to get home.

I guess I'll just walk, she thought to herself as the elevator chimed and the push of the people from the back moved her forward. She pulled her waterproof trench coat tightly around her waist and pulled the hood over her head as she dipped her head and walked through the crowds. She had to get to the over side of the square to take the short cut home. Even without the rain, a walk home would take an hour, and she knew that her shoes would be soaked through by the time she made her way to the other side of the square. She didn't dare think about how ruined they'd be by the time she got home.

"Watch it," came an angry voice to which she ignored, hoping that it wasn't directed at her.

She didn't have the care to turn around and have it out with him, and so decided just to keep walking, hoping to get far away from the angry lines of cold and wet people. Nadia pushed her way through, sighing with relief when she made it to the clearing on the other side and stopped to turn and look at the mass of bodies behind her. Breathing deeply, Nadia decided to take her shoes off and place them in a bag within her work handbag, hoping to preserve them as best she could. Turning back to continue her walk home, she numbed her mind as she walked. She wasn't interested in being in this place anymore; she only wanted to get home. The home where her stuffies waited for her, where she could watch the shows her soul craved and eat snacks that made no sense in the world she was so quickly trying to escape.

I wonder if people look at me and see it, see what I truly desire, she thought, turning a corner and continuing to walk. The rain had chilled her bones to the core, and she shivered as she walked. Her hair falling flat against her head, she took out a hair tie to make a top bun hoping to look slightly more presentable.

I must look so disheveled right now, Nadia almost said out loud, finding herself smirking as she walked around the various puddles on the street and crossing the road, that's when she saw him. Standing against a lamppost, vaping into the rain, his hair slicked back as he ran his fingers through it, seemingly unaware of the storm which thundered around him. Nadia looked at him, standing there, watching as the world turned and wondered how peaceful it must be to remain so calm amid a city in chaos. As if reading her mind, he turned to look at her, smiling as though he had known her for years. Nadia looked away, not wanting to talk to anybody, let alone a strange man but as she slowly looked back at him, she saw that his gaze had not shifted. Nadia smiled back, hoping that a simple smile would satisfy his need for her attention and when he tilted his head at her slowly, she turned the corner and tried to hide the smile which she found to be growing on her face.

"Miss?" Nadia heard him calling after her.

Great, just what I was hoping to avoid, Nadia thought as she turned around.

"You dropped this," he said, holding out her scarf. It was as though the world had stopped turning, and she only saw him. His raven black hair, and blue eyes, his defined jawline, and energy she knew she would be drunk on if she stayed too long.

"Oh, thanks," she replied, reaching out to take the scarf which she tied back onto her bag. Nadia could tell he wanted to talk some more, his twitching lips gave him away, but as she raised an eyebrow, she liked how he decided to let go of whatever he had found so pressing.

"Bye," Nadia said, trying to give him a hint and watched as he took a step back and smiled his knowing smile again before disappearing out of sight.

Weird, she thought, turning around as well and continued the three blocks until she was home.

Nadia opened her door and dropped everything in the doorway as she walked into the bathroom, turned on the shower and crept the hot water up slowly as she warmed her body with each turn on the tap. She had wished she could stop thinking about the guy with her scarf, how his hand been soft and his nails manicured, his face clean-shaven and his business suit soaked through and clinging to his solid form. Leaving the shower, she wrapped her body in her fluffy pink towel, surprising herself as she thought how he would feel holding her as she walked into her bedroom, knowing that she would have to diaper herself for another evening.

Going to her drawer, she took out the pink onesie with the frills on the sleeve, took her blankie and bunny and crawled to the sofa before she put on the movie. Sighing, Nadia fell into her little space as she fell asleep, curled up in a cocoon of blankie and big soft pillows, happy to finally escape the day.

Nadia woke up with a fright, having to remind herself where she was as the house was in complete darkness. She reached for the phone she had left it on the side table next to her sofa and checked the time. It was past midnight as the screen blinded her with its bright background, and as she remembered that she had left her wet clothes on the tiled entrance, she sighed and got up. She walked over to the mess she had left behind, taking her clothes to the laundry and putting them in the washing machine before going to the kitchen and putting some frozen snacks in the oven. She crawled back over to her nest on the sofa and snuggled in as she looked through her handbag and took out her shoes and it was then that she saw the note the man had slipped into her bag when he had handed the scarf back. It was his business card.

Typical, she thought to herself, rolling her eyes as she turned the card over to see something a little more personal.

I know it's a bit of a cliché, but if you'd like to

get to know me, I'll be having coffee at 9:30 Saturday morning at café 86, Jason, the back of the card read.

Well, that is awfully bold of him, Nadia thought trying not to smirk and put the card down. She was hungry, and although his note was intriguing, her dino nuggies really did take priority.

Nadia spent the rest of the week thinking about Saturday, if she would go or if she would just sit at another table and watch him.

He might have given that card out to heaps of girls; Nadia thought as she ate her lunch in the back room at work Friday afternoon. She looked at the expensive bags and munched on her salad as she looked at the colors of the bags she knew she would never be able to afford. Nadia flipped a coin and chose heads to go and tails to stay at home, watching as the coin flipped in the air, she caught it and placed it on the back of her hand. Heads.

Guess I'm having coffee with Jason, she

thought to herself, finished the last mouthful of salad and smiled, excited to be meeting him in less than 24 hours.

Nadia had arrived at the café 15 minutes early and looked out for him.

This might be the dumbest thing you have ever done; she thought as she waited for him and shook her head and laughed in disbelief as he sat down and smiled back at her when he saw Nadia sitting in the café.

"I'm so glad you came!" He said taking the paper napkin and flamboyantly placed it over his lap before looking at her expectantly.

"I'm Jason," he said, extending his hand and offering it to her. Nadia rolled her eyes, and with playful reluctance shook his hand.

"I'm Nadia," she said, as the waitress come to the table. Nadia ordered a peppermint mocha with extra sprinkles, and as she watched the woman walk away, all she wished was that the waitress would come back with her order so she could hide behind the cup.

"So, do you do that a lot?" Nadia asked, wanting to fill the silence that had begun to fall between them.

"Actually, no. But when I saw you a few days ago, I thought, I need to talk to this woman," Jason said as his coffee arrived in front of him. Nadia looked at him, he was perfect, and she couldn't believe that she was sitting with him in this place.

"Well, I hope you aren't a serial killer or something. That would really piss me off because there's this handbag that I'm saving really hard to buy. So, let me have the success of buying it before you know, you chop me up," Nadia half-joked, clutching the warm cup of drink that the busty waitress had only just placed in front of her.

"I'm not a serial killer, but I like your drive. Tell me about the handbag," Jason said, making her laugh.

"You don't want to hear about that," she said, shaking her head and taking a sip of the warm sweet liquid.

"Yes, I do actually," Jason said gently, making Nadia laugh and look at him suspiciously.

"Ok, here it is," she said, opening her phone and showing him the photo of her dream bag. Jason spent a lot of time looking at the photo, making Nadia wonder what he was thinking. When he finally looked up, he looked at her with a seriousness she had seen in most of the men she had dated, almost making her disappointed that he resembled them.

"So, what's your budget like, because if you want that bag, you could have it very easily," Jason said, finishing his coffee in one gulp.

"Um, my budget?" Nadia asked. She had been with financial doms before, but they had always let her down so swinging to the opposite extreme, she lived somewhat paycheck to paycheck.

"Yeah. You don't have one, do you?" Jason asked knowingly. Nadia just shrugged her shoulders and looked out the window.

"Hey, I'm not chipping you. I want to help you," Jason said softly, reaching out to touch her hand.

"Why?" She questioned angrily feeling judged and vulnerable and pulling her hand away.

"Because I'm drawn to you, Nadia. I can't explain it; I just want to be around you and help you have the best life you can," Jason said. She grimaced at him, unable to process what was being said to me.

"Then ask me out on a real date," she asked, waiting for him expectantly, but he just shook his head.

"No. You ask me. Because I've already chosen you, so, if you want me, you'll have to choose me too. Maybe we should," he began to say, but all she heard was the noise in her mind. The piercing scream from all the places she kept locked away and out of reach. Her mind always went there. More than she wished it would. It was exhausting, and yet it was in the exhaustion she had learned to feel peace. Maybe it wasn't even peace she was feeling; maybe it was just her body being too fractured to continue, and in the silence and surrender she could at least be still.

"Dude, I met you like five minutes ago, chill," Nadia said gesturing dramatically, coming back into the room and distancing herself from him. Jason just smirked and nodded before looking out the window to the people on the street.

Chapter 2

"The aquarium? That's where you want to go?" Jason asked, surprised that Nadia had called him and was deep in, organizing a date, mode late Thursday afternoon of the following week.

"Yep. Do you want to come or not?" She asked, keeping her guard up. She had been with guys like him before. The beautiful ones, the ones who knew how desirable they were and was cautious not to make the same mistake with him she had made with other men.

"Alright then, I'll pick you up at 9? Maybe after we could get brunch?" Jason suggested. Nadia just looked from side to side in her living room, unsure if this was a good idea or not.

"I'm good; I'll meet you out the front of the aquarium at 9 o'clock on Saturday. Ok bye," she said before quickly hanging up. She threw her phone onto the sofa and brought her knees to her chest, hyperventilating and staring into space. Happy she was taking a chance on him, but nervous as hell. Deciding she should go for a run, Nadia got up and walked to her cupboard and looked at her little things, wondering how long she would entertain the idea of Jason before sharing with him one of the essential parts of her life. She pushed the thought from her mind and pulled on her activewear, tieing her hair in a messy ponytail and tearing the skin from her cuticle as she walked out the door enjoying the pain and watching as blood pooled along her nailbed. Tensing her calves as the elevator levels flashed on the display screen, Nadia exhaled deeply as two people got into the lift on the 3rd floor. She was happy she had her earphones in her ears so they wouldn't talk to her but returned their smile before looking up at the ceiling.

We need to stop teaching people these bullshit cultural gestures, that's one more smile I'm never getting back, Nadia bitterly thought to herself as she exited the lift and ran from the building not wanting to have to share the space with the friendly strangers for another moment.

She ran like a Brumby from a paddock, letting the cold night air choke her throat as she reminded herself that life was temporary, nothing more or less than moments in time. She hid behind the dark shades that filled the night's sky as she fought back, her tears feeling herself try to run away from the gentlest of monsters who had reached in and ripped the innocence from her soul. The warmth of where his hands had been on her body; still present and never fading. The face that Nadia saw, haunting her as she closed her eyes to fall asleep at night alone and lonely despite her bed almost always being full. The smile Nadia wished she could see again but wanting more than anything she could forget. She frowned as she panted, annoyed that she didn't have a better strategy to numb her pain. She felt like she had never stopped running. It tired her body, but it was her mind she was so desperately trying to silence. It helped her stop thinking when she gasped for air just trying to stay conscious. She tried to say his name as she ran, but the word refused to escape her lips. She could only refer to her nightmare as *him*. So she ran, feeling her body fueled by pain and rage and the memory of a thousand lives she had tried to live since then. And yet, in a moment of remembrance, she was back there. With his body behind her's, whispering in her ear how her body was made for fucking as he slowly felt her under her baby pink pajama shorts.

Goosebumps made her shiver as he kissed the bare tanned skin her white racerback singlet exposed. It had all been so exciting until it wasn't. She remembered how she had liked the noticeable change in the air when she had first seen him and how that mighty wind had stayed for several days after. From a gentle breeze, it grew into a fierce and frightening wind. From swaying trees so peaceful and calm to a violent shaking, daring the branches to bend to breaking point. From trees that were full but filled with nothing but death, to being stripped bare yet only life was left on their branches. The wind was him. Destroying anything that stopped him from what his desires were with relentless ambition, refusing to surrender. Everything about him reflected in one of natures most catastrophically dangerous and uniquely beautiful elements. It didn't surprise Nadia that she had given into him.

How do you refuse a force that exposes your vulnerabilities yet keeps you completely safe from harm? Nadia thought as she doubled over and pulled air from the bottom of her lungs, dry reaching as she remembered how he whispered, *shh Daddy's got you baby girl* when she whimpered and tried to pull away from him.

Was I ever even safe, though, like, this shit doesn't feel very fucking safe, it's ruined my whole fucking life. Was it all just a play to get what he wanted? Did he know that I wouldn't put up a fight? Did he see how my eyes begged to be held? Why do they have the same look in them after all this time? She questioned angrily, knowing that answers to her questions would never be answered. Nadia stood back up and tasted the blood from her dry mouth as she tried to stop the dizziness taking over her body.

He never gave a shit about you; you get that right? You were just something to do, something to pass the time. And you did all that, everything he asked, for what? A fucking hug? Cause Mommy and Daddy fought? Cause no one ever tucked you in at night? Cause there was no one there when you cried when you scraped your knee? Shit. Grow up, bitch. Do you know how much easier life would have been if you just like, weren't so fucking needy? Weren't such a slut, just so fucking easy? Nadia felt her heart whine as she dipped her head and raced up a hill. With him, Nadia saw a reality she had only ever seen in her wildest dreams.

Maybe Jason won't be like, him? Perhaps I was just too young when he showed me all this. Maybe Jason won't ask for so much? Maybe it won't be as bad, maybe he isn't even into this, and I'm just wasting my time, Nadia almost said out loud as she broke back into a military paced run.

It would have been so much easier if it was anyone but him. Why can't I shake this when it's everything but right? Why does it have such a hold over me? Why do I still feel his touch when it was years ago? Why does my body still shiver with anticipation when I think of his hand on my tummy, holding me in place? Was I always going to like this, always into this? Or do I only like it because he showed it to me? Nadia thought, wishing she hadn't seen him every day for the next three and a half years.

She tortured herself as she regretted not being able to prove she was the woman society had raised her to be. She was stuck with the memory, the sadness, the wetness, and the shame. Replaying on constant repeat all the acts she had performed that proved she just wasn't the same as the other girls she had grown up with. It would have been nice to be someone like them. But that just wasn't her. The invisible lines Nadia had circled around herself to stay confined, controlled, socially accepted, and tamed had been ripped open and left bare by him. And as Nadia felt the power he still had over her flooding her senses, she knew all too well, what that sweet, wicked smile of Jason's meant.

"Whatever, fuck it. Never again, straight up, never again will I let someone treat me like that. And if that means I never have a Daddy again and only have some quick turn over, pretend relationship, then so fucking be it," Nadia said out loud as she walked into her apartment building deciding that it was better to be alone than ever feel the need of wanting someone ever again.

"I was starting to think you stood me up," Jason joked as Nadia walked quickly to meet him.

"Yeah sorry, something came up," she said, putting her hands in her pockets.

"What?" Jason asked, making Nadia bite her bottom lip.

"I said something came up," she repeated, unsure why he was smiling.

"Yeah I know, what came up?" He asked, causing Nadia to pulled an annoyed face.

"What are you? A detective?" She replied defensively, only causing Jason to laugh.

"No, I just want to get to know you, you look good," he replied, walking with Nadia as she began to enter the aquarium.

"I get that a lot, try something else," Nadia said, instantly irritated by his eagerness.

"Well, how about this? You are beautiful when you're angry," Jason teased, his face going from smoulderingly alluring to stupid puppy dog in an instant making Nadia stop and turn to look at him.

This is a complete waste of my time, Nadia thought as she looked him dead in the eye.

"Look. This isn't going to happen. Don't follow me. Sorry, take care," she replied, leaving him standing next to a big fish hanging from the ceiling in the foyer. Walking out, Nadia breathed in surrender to her feelings as she began to walk home, happy that Jason hadn't bothered to follow her.

I think I stunned him; she thought as she blocked his number. Walking through the city, Nadia tried to feel anything but the breaking of her heart.

Maybe he would have been nice; perhaps he would have been everything I want, she thought as she haled a taxi. Rolling her eyes, she exhaled and shook her head as she looked up the roof of the smoke-smelling cab. She told the driver her address and slumped down in the backseat, tears escaping her eyes, wishing she could outrun herself. She didn't even really know what she was crying for; all she knew was that it hurt. In the center of her chest like someone had punched and winded her, it hurt. The words past lovers had shared as their parting message, sticking to her like glue. That she was cold, detached, unapproachable, so beautiful but angry, Nadia loved that one the most.

Yeah, I'm fucking angry you dumb fucks, she thought to herself.

How can I not be? You don't fucking know what it's like as much as you all like to pretend you do, she added remembering how everyone had been so devoted to her recovery until they realized that she would never be the girl they wished she was, as the taxi stopped and pulled up outside her door.

Chapter 3

Nadia stayed in bed for the rest of the day, deep in her little space as she tried to numb her pain.

This shit is getting old, she thought, angry that she hadn't figured out how to shake the heavy blackness that lay like a blanket over her.

All I want is a Daddy who will love me. I didn't think that was so hard to ask for, she thought, stripping out of her onesie and diaper and going to the shower.

Running the hot water over her body, she placed both hands on the shower wall, dipped her head, and cried as the water scorched her skinny frame. She yelled, knowing that once again, no one would be able to hear her.

Getting out, she walked naked through the living room and into the kitchen, took an apple slice from her unicorn container and then went back to her room, getting dressed in adult pajamas just as a knock came from the door. Hesitantly, she walked to it, putting the chain in the lock and opening it slowly.

"Hey, I've just moved in next door, and I heard yelling or something coming from here, are you ok?" A man softly said as he dipped his head down to try and meet Nadia's gaze. She was busy looking at his shoes.

Crocodile leather boots, Nadia thought, impressed with his choice and slowly lifting her head. Taking in the man's black wrangler jeans and his green button-down shirt, his eyes kind and gentle and his hair thick and wavey.

"Oh yeah, sorry, I hadn't realized that anyone had moved in yet," Nadia said, feeling embarrassed standing in front of him in her pajamas. He continued to stare at her until Nadia become uncomfortable and shifted her gaze from left to right.

"What do you want?" She softly asked, wanting him to stop looking at her.

"Nothing, my name is Dan, if you need anything, you can always come and ask. Have a good night," Dan said, turning to go back into his apartment.

"Dan, I'm Nadia," she quickly said as he reached his door. Turning around, Dan looked at her plainly, giving her a half-smile and tipping his head slightly before opening his door and shutting it behind him.

Shit, Nadia thought, closing her door and biting her bottom lip.

Well, he heard you, she amusingly said to herself as she started to tidy up her toys.

Over the next three weeks, Nadia had seen Dan four times in the lift, at the local supermarket and had even run into him at her work. He had been looking for a new business suit, and she had directed him to the most expensive suits in the store.

"I know what you are doing," Dan said, smiling in the mirror as he tried on the jacket.

Nadia just rolled her eye dramatically.

"Come on, help a girl out," She just laughed back, happy when Dan passed her his card.

"Well, better go ring these up then," he said, passing her the jacket, matching trousers and shirt and walking back into the changing room with only his own jeans on, his bare chest catching more eyes than just Nadia's.

Oh my god, he is beautiful, she thought walking away to the cash register and waiting for him to come back.

"Hey, Nadia, look I know you're going to want to say no, but," he said pausing to look at her. He saw how she was already thinking of a way to get out of what he was about to say, so he just smiled and shook his head.

"No, what, tell me," she said, seeing how he gave up on her but not wanting him to.

"There's an art gallery opening in town tomorrow night. I want to go, but these things can be so, pretentious, it's nice to have someone there to, you know, fight off the snobby art people. They also make for excellent entertainment and people watching," Dan said, happy to see the smile spread across Nadia's lips.

"You sold it just right, what time?" She asked, surprising herself at how open and excited she was to be spending the evening with him. Dan gestured for the piece of paper behind the counter and took out a pen from his pocket before writing down the address and a time.

"I'll meet you there, see you later," he said, taking the suit bag Nadia bought around to the front of the counter, smiling despite herself and desperate to see him again.

She raced home as fast as she could and took her time searching through the photos of the art gallery looking at the type of dresses other women wore to events like this. Deciding to go with a pink, backless cocktail dress with silver strappy heels, Nadia laid the outfit on her sofa and went to bed feeling the anticipation of having all of Dan's attention.

"Wow, look at you," he said as he saw her walk up to the door of the quaint gallery. She had to stop herself from blushing at his compliment and saw that he was wearing the pants to the suit he had bought the day earlier.

"Nice pants, someone dressed you well," Nadia replied, stopping to kiss him on the cheek before she could stop herself.

Fuck, I hope that was ok, she thought to herself in a panic and slowly stepped back to look at Dan.

"Soft lips," was all he said as he held out his hand to her and walked her inside.

"So, are we pretending to be a loving power couple?" Nadia teased as Dan took two glasses of champagne from the tray that passed them and offered her a glass. Accepting, they made a silent toast before Dan eyed her suspiciously as he took a sip.

"If you'd like. But I was thinking of something a little more. Baby," Dan said, whispering the word baby in Nadia's ear and almost making her choke. She looked up at him with fear in her eyes, clearly not hiding as well as she had thought she had. Dan just held her gaze, blocking her way when she tried to leave.

"Don't run away. There's nowhere to go. You'll have to talk to me like a big girl for a moment," he said, watching how Nadia tried to find a way to escape.

"What do you want? A fucking medal for figuring it out? It's hardly that exciting," she aggressively said, downing her drink and placing the glass on the next tray which passed. Dan just smirked and slowly walked out of the gallery, causing Nadia to stand alone in the room full of strangers before chasing after him.

"Wait," she said, once they were alone on the street. Dan stopped and turned around, kindness pouring from his eyes.

"How did you know?" She curiously asked, coming to stand next to him before grabbing his hand and leading him into the nearest bar she could find. Dan let her lead, finding it endearing that she was trying so hard to face something she was clearly uncomfortable enjoying.

"Are you sure you want to know?" Dan asked, sitting down at a dirty table, making him laugh at how badly they stood out compared to the other patrons who sat around, looking at the way Nadia was dressed. Nadia nodded her head and waited patiently for Dan to order two beers before coming back to sit next to her. Placing the drinks down on the table, he ran his fingers through his hair and thought for a moment before speaking.

"It's the way you feel. I can just tell. You're hurting, badly, and I think you keep that little space right behind the wall you use to block out the world because it all just feels so overwhelming and simply too, everything," Dan said, instantly annoying Nadia who hated how easily he had read her.

"Whatever," she said, rolling her eyes and wishing that she could let herself go and relax for once.

"See?" Dan teased, making Nadia roll her

eyes as she drank the beer in silence.

"You want to go home?" Dan asked, seeing that Nadia was feeling restless. She just nodded, not knowing how to place herself or what headspace to be in, her world felt as though it was spinning, and she couldn't seem to find a feeling to hold onto.

"It's alright Nadia, I'm not going to hurt you, you can trust me," Dan said, opening a taxi door and waiting for her to get in first. She just grimaced at his words and held her breath as she gave him a chance, hoping with all she had that he would be true to his word.

"Do you want to come inside for a drink?" He asked as the city lights rushed past them. Nadia just shrugged her shoulders. She had not been this close to a guy in years. Usually, she would have been long gone by now, and it frightened her to be so physically close to someone.

"I don't know," she said, hoping that he would leave due to her indecisiveness, but Dan just gently smiled at her, slowly reached for her hand and gazed at her in the most unthreatening of ways.

"How about, I just leave my door open and if you want to come in, you can and then if you want to leave, of course, you can do that too," he suggested, making Nadia nod her head as the taxi pulled up outside their apartment building. Dan paid the man and rushed over to Nadia's side as she entered the building. As they reached the elevator, Nadia silently reached for Dan's hand and held it loosely as the lights flicked in ascending order until they stopped on level 10.

"Well, I'll see you if I see you," he said, letting her hand go lovingly before opening his door and walking inside, leaving it open for Nadia who looked in. From what she could see, he had polished concrete floors, white walls with sizeable colorful artwork hanging prominently, and a modern kitchen. Nadia found herself wondering what the rest of his place looked like as she moved towards his doorway and rested against the wall.

"Woah, nice," she involuntarily said as she

looked into the living room and saw the generous leather couches and soft rug in the middle of the floor.

"Your ceilings look higher than mine," she added with a frown. Dan just laughed as he watched her from the kitchen. He had made hot chocolate for both of them and placed the cup on the kitchen counter for Nadia.

"It's just the placing of the furniture. Here, would you like some marshmallows?" Dan said, holding the cup up to Nadia who shifted nervously in the doorway, backing away slowly.

"No, I didn't see you make it, I have no idea what's in there," Nadia said, finding herself feel more confident. Dan just tilted his head, the thought of hurting Nadia had never crossed his mind, but finding out that it had clearly crossed hers, he thought for a moment, watching as her eyes remained unwavering in her decision.

It must be so stressful being a woman and having to be on the highest of guards all the time; he thought as he nodded his head and tipped it down the sink.

"Well, how about you watch me make this one then?" He suggested, seeing Nadia walk into the living room and stopping by the couches. She just nodded her head, and meekly smiled at him as she rested her head on her hands and watched.

"First I'll warm the milk, I just used normal full cream, but I have almond if you prefer," Dan said, opening the fridge.

"Almond, cows milk freaks me out, like just no," Nadia said, making Dan laugh.

"I feel like I should have just known," he said, taking out a mug.

"Now I'm going to heat it," he continued, stopping when Nadia shook her head.

"You have to put the chocolate in next," Nadia corrected as Dan looked at her in confusion.

"Trust me," she added, watching how he soften and followed her instructions.

"Now you heat it," she said when she was satisfied with the level of chocolate Dan had scooped into the mug.

"You'll give yourself diabetes if this is how you take your hot chocolate," he laughed as he waited for the microwave to count down to zero and beep. Taking it out, he stirred it before taking out two marshmallows only to have Nadia have a mild panic attack and race over to the kitchen where he was standing and take the two pink ones from his hands.

"They don't taste nice, I only like the white ones," she said, finding two white ones for the drink and two for her trip back to the couch. Dan laughed, bringing their drinks over to where she stood and sat down on the couch. Dan looked at her, assuming that she would sit but seeing that she remained standing, he stood up again.

"I have never experienced anyone quite like you Nadia," he laughed, sipping his drink.

"White marshmallows are not a game. Honestly, I don't know why they bother making any other flavor," Nadia laughed, feeling more relaxed and deciding to sit, sitting cross-legged on the couch facing Dan who joined her.

"Is this the part where we make small talk?" Nadia said in a voice that made Dan smile.

"I don't care about small talk, and I don't care about talking at all if you don't want to. But if you do want to fill the silence, why don't you ask me some questions," Dan said, leaning into the couch. Nadia just looked at him and wondered how she had been so lucky to have his attention. She knew she wasn't easy to get along with, everyone had always told her how awful she was, but he didn't seem to mind her defenses. He didn't take it personally as everyone else had. They had wanted her trust, her affection, her obedience with only a command to be given, without having earned it, without asking her if she had even wanted them.

Nadia let the silence build between the two of them long after their drinks were finished before speaking again.

"Tell me about this piece. You sold me on a night full of art gazing, and all that I got was a glass of average champagne," Nadia playfully said as she got up and walked to the artwork which hung in the corridor. Dan stayed sitting on the couch, stretched his arms out, and rested his head back.

"It's a piece I did in high school. It feels about 500 years ago now, but we had to do self-portraits. Everyone did their face, but I even in the whirlwind of my 17-year-old self, I knew that my face was not who I was, so I tried to paint my soul. I failed senior art because of it, but it didn't bother me because I knew I hadn't really failed, I had just failed the system that I was being assessed in. It is one of my proudest accomplishments," Dan said, opening his eyes again to see Nadia standing in front of him.

"That's a lot deeper than I thought you'd be," she said, sitting down next to him. He tried to hide the excitement in his eyes at how close she was, but his toothy smile gave him away, causing Nadia to roll her eyes.

"I guess I can surprise you too li," he said, stopping himself from calling her little one. She seemed to be aware of the words he wanted to speak because she just smiled to the side and looked down before looking back up at him.

"You can you know," she said softly, hoping she had read him right.

"What," he said, matching her softness.

"Call me little one," Nadia hesitantly said, biting her bottom lip nervously. Dan just smiled and opened his arms to her and watched as she slowly came closer until her body pressed against his in a loving embrace.

"You are everything you think you're not darling," he said, feeling Nadia's body relaxing slowly in his arms. She closed her eyes to try and stop the tears from escaping her eyes as Dan thumbed them away.

"You're alright, nothing bad will happen to you when you're with me. I'm not going to hurt you," he gently said, rocking her slightly as she cried.

Chapter 4

"I wasn't expecting to hear from you so soon little one," Dan said down the phone the following day. He and Nadia had said goodnight in the early hours of the morning and had only been apart for a few hours when his phone had lit up.

"Yeah, I hope you don't think I'm too clingy or whatever?" Nadia said, concerned that he didn't want to talk to her so soon.

"Not at all, what are you up too?" He asked, hearing Nadia sigh down the phone as she got comfortable.

"I've been thinking about what you said last night, how you suggested that we see if this is something that could work for both of us. I'd like to try," she said, holding her breath. It had been hard enough for her to summon the courage to ring him; she really hoped that he wouldn't deny her request.

"I'd love that!" Dan exclaimed, catching Nadia off guard and making her giggle with excitement.

"Cool," she said, unsure of what to say but wanting Dan to know that she was still interested in the conversation.

"Yeah, it is. So, would you like to go somewhere and talk about a few things?" He suggested, walking to the kitchen and taking a pen and notepad from the top drawer.

"Ok, um, do you want to come to mine, I've seen your place, so it's only fair," Nadia said, happy when she heard Dan laugh.

"Yes, and I fully plan to tell you how to make my coffee to return the favor of your instructions from last night," he teased, making Nadia smile and look around her apartment. She had cleaned it in anticipation for his arrival.

"When are you free?" Dan said, interrupting her train of thought.

"Um, like now?" Nadia laughed, hearing

Dan's door open. She rushed to the door, opening it up to see him standing in his pajama's still on the phone.

"I'm not ready yet," he laughed. Nadia liked how playful he was and tilted her head as she looked at his pajama's. His grey sweat pants and tight white t-shirt made his chest muscles look even bigger than they were.

"Wait there," Nadia said before running back into her apartment, leaving the door open and quickly changing into her pajama's. She wore short red shorts and a grey racerback singlet, the thin straps of her red bra showing against the newly toned muscles of her back. Coming back to where Dan was waiting patiently, he laughed as he saw her.

"Cute," he said, looking at her with a gleam in his eye.

"We can have a pajama party," Nadia said, smiling as she hung up the phone and waved for Dan to come over.

"Alright alright," Dan said, looking around

her place. She had designed her house with a rustic country flare, a cowhide rug on the living room floor and a large white fabric sofa with European pillows making it look like the white marshmallows of her hot chocolate from the previous night. A fluffy pink throw hung over the side of the sofa, and her kitchen looked like something from a magazine. The modern country fixtures made her place look warm and homely, and as Dan stood in front of the wall covered in black and white photos in pinewood frames, he saw the moments of her life.

"This is lovely," he said, turning back around to face her.

"Thanks," she replied, standing in the kitchen by the coffee machine.

"How'd you like it?" Nadia asked, looking at Dan expectantly. He just chuckled as he walked over and stood next to her.

"Well, first off, I like the milk to go in first," he said, shaking his head when Nadia tried to speak.

"No no, I told you I would show you how I like it," Dan said playfully.

"But that's backward," Nadia replied, rolling her eyes. Dan just raised an eyebrow and waited for her to follow his instructions. As she did, he came around the front of the counter and watched her from the barstool.

"Next, I like the chocolate sprinkles," he said, trying to keep a straight face.

"You are legit just making this up as you go along now," Nadia said, as Dan passed her the vanilla syrup.

"And then two teaspoons of this," he said and went to get her the teaspoon. She stirred in the syrup and looked at him dramatically.

"And now the coffee, just you wait, you've never tasted it so good before," Dan reassured her as she just rolled her eyes and poured the coffee in. Passing it to him, he took a dramatic sip before giving it to her.

"Here, try it," he said, nodding his head. Taking the cup in both her hands, Nadia lifted it to her lips and was surprised by how smooth and creamy the drink was, her eyes popping as she looked at Dan.

"Oh my god, how? I've made vanilla lattes before, and they never taste this good. I better make another one," Nadia said, putting the cup back down.

"Because I've drunk yours," she laughed, going to the cupboard and taking out another cup. Dan laughed in surprise.

"I don't know how I feel about that," he said, shocked that she had finished his drink.

"You are a sneaky one Nadia," he said with a smile as he tucked the information away in the back of his mind.

"What sort of things should we talk about?" Nadia said, bringing over the drink she had just made him and gesturing that they should sit on the sofa. Dan followed as he watched her muscled bare thighs and ass and felt his cock wanting to rip her shorts off and bury himself inside of her.

"How into it are you?" Dan said, sitting

down and placing a pillow on the floor. Nadia just looked at him and blushed.

"Um," she said, unsure of how to answer the question.

"Ok, how about I just say stuff, and you say yes or no?" Dan said, seeing Nadia go shy but nodding her head.

"Alright. This will be like 20 questions. Diapers?" Dan said making Nadia bite her bottom lip and nod her head.

"Do you use them or just like being in them?" He added, sipping his coffee.

"Just being in them, but not all the time," Nadia replied softly. Dan smiled and opened his arms to her as he had done the previous night and watched as she hurried over to his side, clinging to him desperately.

"I'm assuming you like to have a paci, blankie, stuffies, and cute clothes?" Dan said as Nadia nodded her response.

"Cute sippy cups and bowls? Bottle feeding?" Dan continued stopping as Nadia stood up and took his hand, leading him into the spare room she had converted into a nursery. Dan looked around the room and smiled at her knowingly.

"Got it," he said, lifting her and holding her in his arms as she placed her head down on his shoulder.

"See, Daddy?" Nadia said, nervously saying Daddy, hoping that Dan wanted to be hers.

"Daddy sees little one," he lovingly replied as he sat down on the rocking chair and rocked her gently.

"I think we are going to be very happy together, baby girl. You're everything that Daddy has been looking for," Dan said, reaching down to the stuffie on the floor and giving Nadia little kisses with it. She didn't believe that she was everything he had been looking for for a moment, and as he sensed her disbelief, he kissed her forehead.

"Why don't you show Daddy which toys are your favorite?" Dan said, gently putting Nadia down on the floor and watching as she crawled over to the large toy box in the corner of the room. She pulled out one stuffie after another, throwing them on the floor behind her until she found the one she was looking for right at the bottom of the wooden box.

"If it's your favorite, what is it doing at the bottom baby girl?" Dan said, sitting on the floor and opening his arms to Nadia who crawled over to him, sitting in his lap and playing with the purple and blue octopus she had just found.

"She's an octy, Daddy, she lives at the bottom of the ocean," Nadia explained to a nodding Dan.

"Oh, I see now little one. What's octy's name?" Dan said stroking Nadia's hair, surprised how deep and quickly she went into her little space.

"Squidly," she replied confidently, holding it up to Dan's face. He just laughed and watched how Nadia played, wondering how their dynamic had changed.

For the rest of the afternoon, Dan and Nadia played, Dan, being introduced to all the little things Nadia enjoyed and seeing how she beamed up at him whenever he called her a good girl. As the night settled in, he yawned, causing Nadia to look at him curiously.

"Daddy, is it your bedtime?" Nadia giggled as she hid behind a toy and her blankie.

"Daddy doesn't have a bedtime, but I bet you do," he replied, checking his watch.

"We better get you some din-dins and a bath now, or you'll be a little grumpy thing," he said, standing up from the coloring in table and accidentally knocking her block tower down.

"Daddy!" Nadia exclaimed, frantically trying to rebuild her construction. Helping her, Dan knelt and followed her instructions for the next half an hour as they rebuilt the masterpiece.

"Alright, that's enough now sweetie," Dan said, lifting her and holding her firmly as he walked her to the kitchen. Placing her down on the wooden chair at the dining table and looked in the fridge.

"What have we got here, sweetie?" He asked more to himself than to Nadia. She just shrugged her shoulders, suddenly seeming to be unaware what the contents of her fridge. Taking out some vegan burgers, tomato, and lettuce, he went to work cooking up healthy burgers. Coming over to the table as Nadia watched him, he placed down the cut-up burger in front of her and fed her as he ate his own.

"Come on little one, just a few more bites," Dan said as Nadia became fussy and refused to eat.

"No Daddy," she said, shaking her head dramatically from side to side.

"No, Daddy?" Dan questioned, making Nadia giggle before looking at him in the eye.

"Didn't you hear about the little girl who said no, Daddy?" He asked, smiling when Nadia excepted another bite. She just chewed politely as her big eyes looked at him.

"She got a spanking, and it hurt so much that she cried. Do you want to cry tonight, baby girl?" Dan asked, finishing off his meal. He saw how Nadia willingly excepted each mouthful he fed her and smiled.

"Well?" He prompted, Nadia quickly shaking her head no and looking at him fearfully.

"I didn't think so. Alright, little lady, let's get you down, and you can play until bath time," Dan said, taking the plates, and cups into the kitchen and tidying up as Nadia crawled around the living room and played with the train set.

Chapter 5

"Trauma is a funny thing," her therapist said at her next appointment. Nadia didn't even know why she was sitting in the room; it's not like anything could be changed. It happened, it all happened, and pretending that something else happened instead was cute for about five minutes. Nadia wanted to yell at the woman sitting in front of her, ask her what she was meant to do at 2 in the morning when she tried to drink herself to ruin. Scream at her for answers as she sat there, listening to a story that she couldn't understand why was being shared.

Why is she so confusing, how has this story got anything to do with me? Nadia questioned, hoping that her eyes wouldn't give her away, the woman already thought she had an attitude, she didn't want to piss her off any more than she already unknowingly had. The last thing she wanted was to have opened up to her just for her to turn around and leave as well. Nadia looked at the wall and wished she could stand up and smash a hole in it, to say that the woman didn't care about her progress, that she didn't care about her at all.

You're just a paycheck, don't forget that, that's all you mean to her. That's all you've ever been, Nadia said as she looked up at the clock on the wall.

Just another pretender, don't forget that she doesn't give a flying fuck about you. You're only here to sort yourself out; she'd lose no sleep if you never woke again just like the rest of them, Nadia told herself as she smiled at the woman who sat in front of her.

"You're angry, that's understandable," the therapist said writing down something making Nadia wish she could read.

No shit, good observation, better write that down too. Nadia is angry that she got fucked up as a kid, Nadia bitterly said to herself as she sat there plainly, unsure of what answer was appropriate.

Why can't you just take it all away? She thought, looking at the woman with all her experience, success, and wisdom.

If you know so fucking much tell me what to do to fix this, I can't feel like this for much longer. Just tell me what you want, what do I need to do to feel better?! Nadia silently screamed, begging from the deepest parts of her soul, wondering if the woman could hear her desperate cry. Nadia looked up as she saw the woman talking but couldn't hear the words she was saying.

I will do anything. Please fix this, please, she begged, defeated and having to surrender to her pain once again as the door closed behind her and she walked out of the office deciding that she needed to go for a run. Trying to shake the emotions that choked her heart, she walked swiftly up the street and towards her apartment. Her breathing coming in shallow gasps as she saw the fog escaping her mouth as the winter night began to cover the city like a wet blanket.

Nadia let the cold air strip her throat as her feet pounded the pavement. This was her escape, her release, her mental health strategy and the only thing that could stop the thoughts in her head from spinning so wildly that she crashed on her bedroom floor and let one panic attack wash over her after another. Deciding that her demise wasn't an option, she routinely pulled herself together for as long as her day demanded. She had been captain of the track team, and led her team to victory, taking them to the state finals. She had the type of beauty that prompted questioning of a modeling career by relatives at family reunions. She was the perfect daughter, successful, courageous, determined, but no one saw who she truly was. She was the one who screamed her broken heart into her pillow until she tasted blood in her throat every night. The one who people loved to be loved by, with leftover innocence freely given to others until they weren't satisfied anymore and discarded her. Leaving her with nothing but a coldness that seemed to creep down her spine and coil around her throat, her heart being glued together with ice.

The coldness had been apart of her for as long as she could remember. It had settled in after that night, the one she didn't want to remember. The one with the guy who had told her that, *Daddy was there,* only to leave her in the morning. A guy who had been the first to show her what gentleness was, the one who had taken her to the surface after she had been drowning for years. She had thought he would have been there after that, he had said he would, but he had left and in his wake given her a working pattern. One where she chose who had her, and when they left. She had blurred the lines, consenting to the things she didn't want to only to try and find something more painful than what he had done to her so that he wasn't the pinnacle of her pain.

"Hey," Dan said, as Nadia turned the corner and ran into him. It was late and dark, and she wasn't expecting to see anyone out on the street, let alone him. She stood in front of him, puffing and wiping the tears from her eyes as she tried to see his image clearly.

"Hi," she replied, taking her earphones off and holding them in her cold hands. Dan just looked at her, with her red lips and cheeks, the first of the evening snow dotting her hair.

"Baby, do you want to walk home with Daddy?" Dan said, immediately feeling Nadia's arms wrapping around his waist and holding onto him like he was the one thing that could keep her from collapsing.

"Shh, there there little one, Daddy's here. Come on, take my hand, let's get you warmed up," he said, taking off his thick felt and fur coat and wrapping it around her shoulders, instantly warming her frozen body. Nadia hadn't realized that she was frozen to her bones until the warmth of Dan's coat gave her pins and needles as she warmed up. Nadia looked at Dan, his navy business suit and tan leather satchel slung over his chest, the silver crest catching Nadia's eye.

"Daddy, what do you do?" She asked, as he loosened his crimson tie and smiled down at her.

"I'm a lawyer baby girl. I'm really impressed that you've got a big girl job," Dan said, as they walked quickly, both wanting to get out of the cold and into their dynamic in the privacy of the apartment.

"It's not that big, I just work in a store," Nadia replied, looking into the windows of the cafes they passed.

"I like that you can look after yourself," Dan said, tilting his head at the expensive activewear which Nadia was wearing. She just giggled and shrugged her shoulder as Dan opened the door to their apartment for her. Climbing the stairs, Nadia took off his coat and handed it back to him before she turned and kissed his cheek.

"Thanks, Daddy. Do you want to come in?" She asked, opening her door.

"Maybe later, but right now I think you should come into my place, let me cook for you and take care of you tonight?" He asked, making Nadia have to think for a moment. She ground her teeth before nodding and shutting her door again before turning back around to him.

"Ok," Nadia softly said, making Dan smile.

"I love that you are giving me a chance. I'll show you that you can trust me," he said opening his door and walking inside, hanging his coat and bag on the hooks at the door before turning around to see that Nadia was standing against the closed door of his apartment. He smiled, took his jacket off, followed by his tie, and walked into his bedroom.

"Do you want to have a shower or bath sweetie? I've got a few things here I think you might like," he called from his room, gaining Nadia's curiosity as she followed the sound of his voice and walked into his bedroom. Looking at the things he placed on his bed, she smiled and walked over to inspect them further.

"Did you get all these for me?" She asked, picking up the star-patterned onesie and bit her lip excitedly.

"Yeah, I wasn't sure which one you would want so I got a few. And these as well," Dan said as he half jogged to the far side of his room and opened the cupboard, taking our three pairs of thigh-high socks which matched the onesies. Nadia gasped and placed both hands on the sides of her face in surprise.

"They are all so pretty, Daddy!" Nadia squealed happily making Dan exhale in delight.

"Oh good, I took some notes from your selection. I'm pleased you like them. So now you can have a bath here because you have jammies to be changed into afterward," Dan said, sitting on the edge of the bed and looking into Nadia's sparkling eyes.

"Can you help me please, Daddy?" Nadia asked, getting stuck in her long sleeve as she tried to pull it over her head. Laughing, Dan stood up, and she held her breath as she felt his hands traced up her toned sides lifting the pink running shirt off her head, looking her gently in the eyes as he sat back down and looked at her standing in front of him in her sports tights and bra.

"Daddy, you make me nervous," Nadia said in her little voice as she began to blush. Shutting his eyes, Dan placed his hands on his knees and raised an eyebrow.

"How about now? Now I can't see you at all," he said, smiling. Nadia quickly took her sneakers and socks off before touching his hands, causing him to open one eye.

"I don't want you to laugh at me," Nadia nervously said, as she rolled her tights down.

"Why would you think I'd laugh at you little one?" Dan said frowning, his eyes filled with nothing but love.

"Because maybe you think I don't look nice," she said, making Dan tilt his head dramatically.

"Baby girl, I think you are the most beautiful girl I have ever seen!" He replied, surprised that she would be self-conscious about her appearance. Nadia had the looks of a woman most men would be too intimidated by even to approach her at a bar. She had the cold eyes that pierced a heart and a stare that rattled the most confident of men, but Dan had known her deal the minute he laid eyes on her.

"Ok, just checking," Nadia said as she stood in front of him only wearing her underwear.

"Coz like, you haven't tried anything with me. So I just don't know, like if you like me or not," Nadia said, looking down at the ground.

"Baby girl, I haven't tried anything because you're my little one. I'd rather keep all the grown-up stuff for when and if you want to have that relationship with me too. But we have only explored this side of us so, that will have to be a conversation we have when you are feeling like a big girl," Dan explained making Nadia smile and nod her head.

"Is that why you've been so nervous around me, coz you think I'm going to do grown-up things to you, little girl?" Dan asked, picking up a onesie and socks and standing up.

"Yeah," Nadia replied, excepting the hand, Dan offered her as he led her into the bathroom.

"Silly girl. I'm not like that. I like to keep both dynamics separate, I like to regress you, age play is fun too, but mostly I'll want to regress you," Dan explained as Nadia stood on the bathmat, the floor heating making the mat warm. Dan placed Nadia's things down on the wooden stool in the corner and ran the shower, wondering if he should leave or take her underwear off or what she wanted him to do.

"Daddy, I need help," Nadia said, turning around before feeling his hands unhooking the clips of her sports bra before she turned back around, letting him see her body for the first time. She slowly pulled down her panties, Dan smiling as he saw her shaved pussy and watched as she got in, under the water.

"What's for dinner, Daddy?" Nadia asked as she showered, Dan watching her model-like body twist and turn under the showerhead.

"I honestly just want a big cheesy pizza. Do

you like that? I can get you whatever you want, what do you want, baby?" Dan said, holding a towel open for Nadia who made happy noises as he dried her.

"Yeah, I like pizza, but I like mine with BBQ steak as well," she said, surprising Dan.

"Alright, we will get two pizza's then," he said, laying her on the floor, the warm tiles feeling strange under her body as she had prepared herself to be cold. Dan took a diaper and powder from the cupboard and gently slapped her thighs, waiting for her to lift up before he slid the diaper under her bottom. Sprinkling powder over her, he fastened the tabs around her body and bent down to kiss her tummy, making Nadia giggle and happily fall even deeper into her little space. She placed her thumb in her mouth as Dan dressed her in the onesie, helping Nadia to roll the sleeves up when he saw her struggle.

"I don't like things touching my wrists, Daddy," Nadia explained, keeping her leg steady as he rolled the socks up her thighs.

"I see," Dan said, sitting back on his hunches, admiring how beautiful and peaceful Nadia looked.

"But I only like long-sleeve onesies. I think the short sleeve ones are yucky," Nadia said giggling.

"Is that so?" Dan replied, picking Nadia up and holding her in his arms like a princess as he walked her through the apartment and into the living room.

"Daddy needs to have a quick shower, baby girl. I'll order our dinner, and it should be ready by the time Daddy is out of the shower, alright?" Nadia just nodded her head and swayed her legs as she sat cross-legged on the couch, waiting as Dan put on a show for her.

"I like this one, Daddy," she said, pointing to the tv as Dan put the remote down on the table.

"Alright, I'll be quick," Dan said, rushing into the shower, knowing that the pizza would be there in about 10 minutes.
Nadia watched the show with the puppies and

their exciting adventures, getting lost in the show and not hearing the first knock at the door. Dan was still in the shower as the second knock came more loudly than the first, starling Nadia and making her turn her head towards the door. As the third knock came, she quickly headed to the shower, stopping and pivoting as yet another knock came making her confused as to what to do.

"My Daddy said I can't open the door," she found herself saying, in her little voice.

"Ok, is your Daddy there? I've got your pizza here," the voice of the pizza delivery girl said on the other side of the door. Nadia just looked around nervously.

"Did he already pay online?" Nadia asked, biting her bottom lip and holding her breath.

"Um, let me see. No, he didn't. I need $20 sweetie," the woman replied, pressing her ear to the door as she heard Nadia scurry away. Nadia went to Dan's bedroom to find his wallet, opening it up and sighing in relief when she saw a 20 dollar bill. Running back to the door, Nadia pushed the note through the gap at the bottom of the door.

"There," she said happily as the woman laughed.

"Thanks, but you'll have to open the door if you want your pizza's," the woman said, making Nadia think.

"It's ok. You can leave it there. Daddy will get it later," Nadia said, running to the bathroom as she heard the shower being turned off.

"Daddy?" She said, peeping her head into the foggy bathroom.

"The pizza is here, I already paid, but she's left it out the front," Nadia said.

"Oh, baby, damn I took a lot longer than I thought I was going to," Dan said, laughing as he wrapped a blue towel around his waist and ran to the door. Opening it, he saw the pizza lady had left the pizza's on his doorstep with a note on top reading, *Sir, you need to take better care of your little girl. Leaving someone so young alone is really not on.* Dan just laughed as he scrunched the note up and threw it in the trash as he plated a slice of

Nadia's pizza for her.

"That was a close call, Daddy!" Nadia said, as she took her slice in both hands and took a huge bite.

"Mmm, yummy," she said, chewing happily, tilting her head from side to side, the happy dance she did when she ate something she enjoyed.

"I know! You were clever to get my wallet," Dan said, smiling at Nadia.

Chapter 6

Nadia had fallen asleep in Dan's arms as they had watched a film, wrapped up in blankets and full of pizza. Opening her eyes, she saw that she was still laying on his couch, but that Dan was nowhere in sight.

"Daddy?" Nadia called through the apartment, hearing a thud coming from the bedroom. Getting up slowly, she sleepily rubbed her eyes and made her way to the bedroom, smiling when she saw Dan.

"Daddy, what are you doing?" Nadia said, watching as Dan jumped around the room trying to put on his sock.

"I overslept, I'm late for work," he laughed. Nadia was happy that he wasn't angry at her, assuming it was her fault he was late.

"Oh sweetie no, it's not your fault," Dan said

as if reading her mind. Nadia just blushed, wondering if she was as obvious to everyone else as she was to Dan.

"I'll be home late today. Are you working?" Dan asked, pulling his pants up. Nadia couldn't help notice his defined muscles as he tucked his shirt into his pants and tightened his belt around his waist.

"No. Daddy, can you change me before you leave. I want to be a big girl again," Nadia asked. Dan stood still for a moment and checked his watch.

"I'm already late, an extra few minutes for my baby girl won't save me. I'm all yours," Dan said, laying Nadia down on the bed and taking her onesie off.

"But Nadia, your work out gear is still dirty," Dan said, curious as to how she would get to her apartment without clothes.

"Then it's a good thing I look so good," she said, winking at him and making Dan have to catch his breath as he saw her transform into the gorgeously seductive woman he knew her to be.

"You little tease," Dan said, looking at her naked, perfect body in front of him.
Dan opened the door to his apartment as he saw Nadia prance around, collecting her things, and coming to the door.

"It's clear," Dan said, enjoying how Nadia lived her life in extremes. Watching as Nadia quickly made her way to her door and opened it just as the elevator chimed and someone walked out. Laughing, Dan winked at Nadia who just smiled back as she slowly shut her door, locking it once it shut.

Oh my god, he's fantastic, Nadia thought to herself as she walked through her apartment, the sun streaming through the windows signaling mid-morning.

Nadia spent the day messaging with Dan. He had gotten away with being so late for work, and they had laughed at how close Nadia had been to getting caught running naked down the corridor of their apartment floor. When he had said he needed to get some work done before his boss became suspicious of his happy mood, Nadia sent him a winky smilie and put her phone in her jeans pocket before getting off the couch.

"He is a dream," she said out loud. It felt like the first time in years when she didn't have to fight herself to feel happy. It just seemed to flow through her veins.

Happiness, Nadia thought, smiling as she decided to go for a walk around the neighborhood. Putting her shoes on and grabbing her coat, she pulled the door shut behind her.

She walked passed the cafés and restaurants. She admired the window displays of the designer boutiques, and although the air was crisp, she enjoyed the warmth of the sun on her face.

"Well, now I know you are stalking me," Dan's voice laughed, making her turn around to see him. She flung her arms around his body and held him tight, nuzzling into him and smelling his cologne.

"What are you doing, lovely?" He asked, stroking her hair out of her face and kissing her forehead.

"I just thought a walk might be good. I've been inside all day," she replied, holding his hand as he led her back down the street.

"Want to get a bite to eat? I'm starving," Dan asked, Nadia just nodding her head. With him, she felt herself go into her little space with the simplest of things. Being called lovely, how he reached for her hand upon seeing her, it was those things that gave her butterflies in her stomach, but that also made her heart explode.

"Are you in the mood for something or can I pick?" He asked.

Even the way he asks still makes him sound like my Daddy, Nadia thought, resting her head on his arm as they walked.

"You can pick," she replied, laughing when they stopped at the next restaurant.

"I've picked. It's the closest one," Dan said, enjoying his decision and walked inside. It was a small sandwich joint, the smell of fries and mustard, making Nadia's stomach rumble.

"Oh, are you hungry little one?" Dan said, giving Nadia a mild heart attack. She looked around nervously, hoping that no one heard him.

"You can't call me that here," she said. Dan just smiled at her as he took her to the seats at the back.

"Are you scared someone will find out you are my beautiful baby girl?" He whispered in her ear, making her shiver.

"Yes, Daddy," Nadia replied, kissing him on the tip of his nose. Dan sat down next to her, and she snuggled into his side as they looked over the menu.

"Nadia? Nadia Harris? Is that you?" A voice said from the counter. Nadia and Dan both turned around to see a man in his mid 40's looking at Nadia. He was a tall man and looked like someone on the Forbes billionaire list. His short grey hair complimented by the navy business suit he wore. Nadia froze, and Dan could feel her heart skip a beat as she looked at the man like a deer in headlights.

"I think you must be mistaken," Dan said, trying to get the man to leave.

"No, I know it's you. I would remember those lips anywhere," the man said, coming over to stand over Nadia, sandwiching her between him and Dan.

"Well, aren't you going to introduce me? I thought I taught you better than that?" The man said, enjoying the discomfort he brought to Nadia. Nadia just looked at the ground, making the man laugh and extend his hand to Dan.

"I'm Rupert, Rupert Sullivan. Nadia and I use to, well, what did we use to do, baby?" Rupert said, making Dan tighten his grip around the older man's hand. Letting go, Dan stood up, meeting the Rupert at eye level.

"You'd better go. It is clear Nadia doesn't want to see you," Dan said, moving Nadia, so she was behind him.

"Well, a baby doesn't know what she wants,

that's why she needs Daddy to tell her," Rupert said, laughing as a tear escaped Nadia's eye. Rupert turned around, collected his order, and left the restaurant, Dan watching him with protective viciousness in his eyes until he was out of sight. Sitting back down, Dan saw that their meal had arrived and Nadia sat frozen in the booth.

"Talk to me sweetie," Dan said, bringing her close as she suddenly burst into tears. He held her, stroked her hair and waited until she pushed him away, looking up at Dan with the saddest eyes he had ever seen.

"I don't want to," Nadia slowly said, looking at the delicious food in front of her and beginning to eat in silence. Dan just looked at her, and although he wanted to have his questions answered, he didn't push the issue with her and bit into his wrap.

Dan paid for the meal, and they left the restaurant, silence, and questions still looming in the air. They had walked a block before Dan looked at Nadia as they waited for the street light to turn green.

"I get that you don't want to talk about it, I just want you to know that whatever that was back there, you aren't losing me," Dan said, feeling Nadia reach for his hand.

"Thanks," she replied, walking across the road, Dan's hand making her feel safe.

"I wouldn't even know where to start," she said, pointing to a park bench, not wanting to go home to sit in her apartment alone. Dan let her lead as she found the bench she liked and sat down. They sat there, watching the world spin around them, Nadia feeling as though she was invisible.

"When I was 18 I ran away from home because it was just too dangerous to be there any longer," Nadia began, remembering how she had learned the hard way to lock herself in the bathroom when her father's friends had come over to drink. Shaking her head, wanting the memory to be gone, she tried to form the words her heart so desperately wanted to speak.

"I ran out of money pretty quickly. I bounced from couch to couch but pretty soon I was on the streets. He found me," Nadia said, feeling the sting of his name on the tip of her tongue. Dan wrapped his arm around Nadia who curled into him, placing her legs over his as she watched the trees in the park rustle.

"Pretty soon I was turning tricks from him, his friends would come over, and I'd be their entertainment. He gave me a place to live, clothes, food. I didn't know how to leave him. So he left me instead," Nadia said, swinging her leg, kicking a stone back and forth as she waited for Dan's reply. She looked up at him, hoping that he still liked her as saw the anger in his face.

"I can't believe some people. I am so sorry that happened to you," he said, making her exhale and rest her head on his arm.

"He was my first Daddy. I didn't know what I was doing, and he was so abusive and cruel. Then one day, I woke up to my bags packed at the door with a note on them saying that if I was still there when he got back, he would call the police," she continued to explain.

"So I just left. I tried to call him, but he had blocked my number, I tried to find him, but when I went back the next day, someone else was moving into his house, and they said that he had left town. I was all on my own again," Nadia said, biting her bottom lip as she tried to hold her tears back.

"I've got you now, darling, and I won't let anything bad happen to you. You'll see," Dan said. Nadia thought she would feel better after sharing her story with Dan, but as they got up to leave, her vision became blurry, a sweat broke out on her forehead, and the color drained from her face as she lunged forward and was sick behind the park bench.

"It's ok, Daddy is here, let it out sweetie," Dan lovingly said as he rubbed her back. Nadia's eyes watered as her stomach emptied itself of the meal she had only just consumed almost as if her body was trying to cleanse itself from the memory she had just dragged up.

"Daddy's got you, come on, baby girl, let me take you home," Dan said, taking out a tissue from his pocket and stopping a peddler and buying Nadia a bottle of water before they left the park.

Chapter 7

Nadia had stayed in bed for five days after seeing Rupert. Dan had been by her side almost the whole time, only going into work once during the week. He had watched her as she slept, her nightmares reoccurring as she relived her past in her dreams.

"It's just a bad dream, little one," Dan said, as Nadia began to stir in her sleep violently. Dan gently shook her awake, holding her hand as she gasped, her eyes popping open, and her heart beating wildly.

"Shh, Daddy is here. You're safe, and nobody is going to hurt you," he said, as she began to cry. She hated this. Not being able to shake the demons that had haunted her for so long they had become a part of who she was. She didn't want to be like this. She wanted to be happy. To be able to love Dan the way she wanted to, freely, without fear of him hurting her or turning on her. She knew in her mind that she could trust him, but her heart was the thing which ruled her life and just like every other time, she felt uncomfortable, it said to run.

"I'm sorry you don't have to be here. I can handle this. I know you've missed a lot of things this week because of me," Nadia said, only stopping because of the paci Dan put in her mouth.

"Shh, little girl. Don't talk about such silly things. You are more important than the jerks at my office," Dan replied, putting a cold towel on Nadia's forehead and patting her left side until she was back asleep.

The following Monday, Nadia got up before Dan, stretching her toes along the wooden floors before walking into the kitchen. This was the first time she had been out of bed for a reason other than using the bathroom. Walking to the coffee machine, she turned it on and waited for the creamy warm liquid to fill her cup. Taking it, she went to sit down on the couch and listened to the birds chirping outside. Closing her eyes, she wondered who she would have been if she had been given a different life. She had longed for someone to rescue her, to save her, and every time someone tried, all she did was push them away. She was grateful to herself for not pushing Dan away. She liked how he had calmed her wild heart, and she loved even more that she let him.

How did I get so lucky, Nadia thought as she saw him run around the corner, worry on his face.

"Baby?!" Dan said, checking her over to make sure everything was alright.

"Daddy?!" Nadia playfully replied. She looked up at him and waited for him to speak.

"Are you ok?" He asked, sitting down next to her when she nodded yes.

"I was worried when you weren't in bed. Why didn't you wake me?" Dan asked, seeing that her coffee cup was empty and placing it on the table.

"Because you've been working overtime on

me and I wanted you to rest, Daddy," she replied, kissing his cheek.

"Such a sweet girl. Can I get you breakfast?" He asked, already knowing what Nadia would like.

"Waffles!" Nadia happily yelled, lifting her arms in the air and getting cuddled by Dan.

"Hey, Nadia?" Dan said, using her name to signal that he wanted to have an adult conversation with her. She just cleared her throat and wriggled from his arms.

"Dan," she replied, suddenly becoming the alpha female he had seen a handful of times.

"I think, maybe going to therapy and getting some professional help for this might be a good idea," he said, catching her off guard.

"Therapy is for people with problems. I don't have problems," she replied, taking the ingredients from the pantry to make waffles. Dan just made himself an espresso and raised an eyebrow at her.

"Fine, I have a slight problem. But I think I'm good now," Nadia said, wanting to end this conversation. Dan just took her hand gently in his and gripped it tightly when she tried to pull away.

"What if I come with you?" He suggested making her roll her eyes.

"What I want to do more than not go to therapy would be to have you there. How creepy, I don't want you to know all this shit, to begin with. Just drop it," Nadia said, hoping that by rejecting Dan's suggestion, she wouldn't lose him.

"I'll drop it, once you go," he said, kissing the tip of her nose and making her laugh and groan knowing that she'd be making that appointment sooner rather than later.

"How is everything going?" Her therapist asked, two days later. Nadia had avoided eye contact for as long as possible, something about the way this therapist looked at her made her feel, seen, and that was deeply uncomfortable.

"Really great," Nadia lied behind a smile.

She can probably figure out I'm lying, look at the way she's staring at me like she already knows,

Nadia thought, looking around the room and not knowing where she was meant to start. Her therapist looked at her expectantly, reading through the front Nadia was so desperately trying to keep from falling.

"Really?" She asked, raising an eyebrow and making Nadia just laugh at her futile attempt actually to be alright.

"No, obviously, I'm sitting here," she said gesturing to the room.

"So why have you come today?" The therapist said. Nadia looked around the room, wondering how fast an hour could go.

"Because my boyfriend said I probably should," Nadia replied, excited to be able to call Dan her boyfriend.

"Why do you think he suggested it?" the woman asked.

Oh great, she's persistent, Nadia thought, annoyed that she was going to have to give this woman something to go with.

"I don't know because I had a rough start?"

Nadia said hoping that was enough.

"Tell me about it," the woman said, causing Nadia to breathe loudly.

"I don't want to," Nadia replied, annoyed that her guard was being taken down so quickly by this stranger with a look on her face like she knew all of Nadia's secrets.

She's got, like super fucking powers or something, she angrily thought, looking at the ground.

"Look, I know you are trying to help and just doing your job, but I really don't want to be here," Nadia said looking at her dead in the eye, slightly unnerved by the unwavering stare she was receiving back. Breaking first, Nadia looked away, annoyed that she didn't feel in control anymore.

"I know you don't want to, but tell me what happened anyway," the woman said, smiling at Nadia, challenging her to be brave. Nadia just smiled a sideward smile, rolled her eyes, and gave a half-laugh, surprised that she suddenly didn't completely hate being in the room and sighed. She bit her bottom lip, annoyed that tears escaped her eyes like a flood breaking as she breathed deeply trying to hold them back.

"It's ok, you're safe here, I'm not going to hurt you," the woman said only making Nadia laugh and shake her head in disbelief as she wiped her tears away.

You probably would have, given the chance. You're probably just like they were. You're all the same. But I'd fucking kill you if you tried now though...or, would I? She thought to herself, seriously contemplating which decision she would make, glad she hadn't let that slip from her lips.

"My father was an abusive drunk. I don't have a mother, and I was homeless when I was 18," Nadia said in one breath, leaning back into the couch. Feeling the roughly put together scabs of her heart being slowly ripped off and the wounds made vulnerable, exposed and bleeding, a pain almost unbearable to allow herself to feel.

Well, that was different, Nadia said on her

walk home. The therapist had said words Nadia didn't know the meaning of and she spent the whole 20-minute walk doing internet search after internet search learning about energy, NLP, and the different levels of hypnotherapy. Walking into Dan's apartment, she put her phone on the kitchen bench and upon seeing him, wrapped her arms around him, kissing him on the mouth.

"Woah, what was that for," he said, surprised at her sudden passion.

"I'm pretty sure this is what happy feels like," Nadia replied, going to the fridge and taking out two beers.

"And I'm also pretty sure I'm about to be drunk," she added, opening both bottles, turning on a country playlist which boomed through the apartment and walked back over to him.

"So it was good then?" Dan asked, as the timer of the dino nuggets chimed, Nadia raising an eyebrow, putting her beer down.

"What's in there?" She suddenly asked, already knowing the answer. Dan just laughed.

"You don't have to have them if you don't want, I just wasn't sure how you'd be when you came back, so I thought it was better to be prepared," he explained. Nadia looked at the beer in her hand and the tray of nuggets in Dan's and just moaned.

"I don't know what I want either!" She said in destress.

"Look, finish the beer, then have the nuggies, and then I'll get you ready for bed, ok?" Dan suggested, Nadia just nodding as she chugged her drink, finishing it before Dan came over with her plate.

"Heaven," she said, happily sighing and eating with her eyes closed.

"I'm glad it was so good, baby," Dan said, taking the beer bottle away and watched as she happy danced as she ate.

"I wonder how long this will last?" Nadia asked when Dan came to sit down next to her.

"What do you mean?" He questioned, pulling her into his lap and smiling at her as she turned in his arms.

"I just hope that this awesome feeling doesn't go away," Nadia said, burying her face into Dan's chest, snuggling with him as he turned off the music and turned on a show.

Nadia knew that she had to go to work the next day, and groaned as her alarm woke her up.

"I just don't think this is normal to be woken up by that noise," she complained as she got up and walked through her apartment, turning on the coffee machine, making a piece of toast and eating it with her eyes closed. She had spent the night in her own apartment, Dan staying in his. She had said that she wanted to see if she could manage a night without him but had tossed and turned the whole night. Unbeknownst to Nadia, Dan had suffered the same fate. She beamed when a knock came from her door, assuming it would be Dan. Opening it excitedly, Nadia dropped her piece of toast when she saw the image that greeted her.

"Hey bunny," Rupert said, standing in front

of her making her forget she was a thriving 27-year-old with a resume that screamed success and abundance. She forgot that she had a man who loved her, she forgot that she had somehow managed to survive all her hardest days and in an instant, she was back there, the girl she had worked so hard to distance herself from.

"Well, aren't you going to let me in? Daddy wants to see how far his good girl has come," Rupert said, stepping forward, making Nadia step back and hold her breath.

"Um, no," she said, the words sounding more like a suggestion than a command making Rupert laugh.

"No? When have you ever said no? I don't remember ever saying that *no* was an option," he said trying to push his way in, Nadia refusing to move. She tensed her calves, reached up and pushed him back, not moving him an inch.

"You'll have to do better than that," he said, lifting his hand to strike her, backhanding her across her face. She let out a high pitched gasp as she fell to the ground, Rupert standing over her, his hands on the front of his belt buckle. Nadia closed her eyes, wishing she could disappear, wishing that she wasn't crying, wishing that he would go away as Dan's door opened.

"The fuck?" Dan said, quickly taking in the situation, dropping his briefcase, placing his hand on Rupert's shoulder and turning him around, ducking the punch Rupert threw before Dan slammed his fist up under Rupert's chin, knocking him back and causing him to cough. Dan's eyes burned with a violence Nadia didn't know he could possess as he walked toward Rupert, blocking his punches and tripping him, straddling his chest and laying his fists into the older mans face until Rupert couldn't open his eyes. His blood spraying across the floor as Dan grabbed the sides of his face only to smash his head back against the floor. Getting up, Rupert unconscious on the floor, Dan went to Nadia who had stood and rested against the wall, having watched the whole thing.

"Baby girl, let Daddy see," Dan said,

becoming the gentle, loving man Nadia knew him to be.

"You're cut, baby, come inside and let me look after that for you," Dan said, picking up his briefcase and placing it just inside his door, before going back and dragging Rupert's body into the corridor and leaving him there.

"I had no idea you could fight like that," Nadia quietly said, as she sat on his kitchen bench and let him put ointment on her cheek.

"I watched my father beat my mother, and I watched her choose him over herself and me every time. She was weak and broken. I told myself I would never be that pathetic, lying to herself about why she should put up with such a crappy life. And as much as I can understand her reasons, hell, I can even understand his reasons for being such a prick, I decided that I needed to heal myself so that I didn't become either of them. I learned how to defend myself early. Then I learned how to love, out of everything, that was the hard part. Something neither of them managed to learn how to do," Dan explained as he placed a bandaid over Nadia's cut.

"There, little one," he said, kissing her forehead and helping her get down.

"I can't go to work like this," Nadia said, attempting to pull the bandaid off.

"Then don't. Let's just, retire. Go do something else. Live a different life. There is nothing particularly interesting about my job. I hate how they take their pound of flesh and give nothing back," Dan said. It was these moments that made Nadia know she loved him. Who else would burn the world down with her until it matched a dream they carried in their hearts.

"Fuck it. I've got some savings. Do you? How long could you go without work?" Nadia said, looking down and realizing that she was still wearing her pajamas. Dan sat on the floor and kicked off his shoes, making Nadia laugh at how he looked with his elegant suit and fancy hair cut, sitting on the floor. Joining him, she crawled into his lap as he took out his phone and dialed a number.

"God, I hadn't registered that I've been waiting for this day. I've got savings too, could probably go about a year without work," he said before quickly becoming serious.

"Good morning, Mark. I'm really sorry, actually, no, I'm not. I'm fucking over the moon to tell you that I won't be coming into work, um, ever again. I quit," Dan said, hanging up the phone and sighing with relief, laying back on the floor and bringing Nadia with him. Breathing as though he had just run a race, Dan's eyes watered, and he let his tears fall from his eyes.

"Thank you, baby girl," he said, kissing her and holding her tight as he relaxed into the floor.

Chapter 8

Dan and Nadia stayed like that until their bodies became numb. Nadia ringing her work and quitting as well. Looking at each other, they both laughed and shook their heads in disbelief.

"Did we actually just do that?!" Nadia squealed, clapping her hands excitedly and jumping up and down.

"I feel free. I hadn't even realized that I had felt so caged. Oh my god, we can do whatever the fuck we want, baby!" He replied, going to the cupboard and pouring a whiskey. Nadia tilted her head left and right, before walking into the kitchen.

"What? There are no rules now. I don't have to turn up to work dead sober, I don't have to wear this fucking leash ever again," Dan said as he loosened the tie around his neck and ripped it from his body. Nadia took the bottle from his hand and took a deep swing, gasping as the liquid burned her throat.

"I don't have to be nice to rude jerks who think that treating retail staff like shit makes them special," Nadia said, placing the bottle down.

"Wanna get day drunk?" Dan said, pouring another glass.

"I kinda think I already am," Nadia laughed as she turned on music and danced around the kitchen.

"But seriously, what do you want to do now?" She asked, stopping suddenly and sitting on the floor. Dan came over with blank paper and the crayons she kept on his office desk and sat down with her.

"Let's design our life," Dan said, sitting next to Nadia who took the pink crayon.

"I kinda like my therapist. She's not what I expected. I'd like to keep seeing her. I think I've still got some stuff to sort out," Nadia said writing that down. Dan just nodded and thought about what he wanted.

"I want to own a bar. I wanted to learn about hospitality until like, I got told not too. Fuck, why did we even listen to anyone but ourselves?" He asked, shaking his head.

"Oh, that's original, a Daddy with a bar. There's actually a bar for sale next to the sandwich store we went to that time. The owner is only selling because he is moving to Jersey," Nadia said, writing down the bar idea next to the therapist.

"So we want to stay in the city?" Dan asked, smiling when Nadia nodded.

"I like it here, you?" She asked, Dan, agreeing eagerly.

"Great. Well, I guess we are moving in together?" Nadia asked, biting her bottom lip and smiling excitedly.

"One thousand percent," Dan said, opening his phone to look at houses for sale.

"I will sell this place. Do you rent or own yours?" He asked, taking an orange crayon and writing *house.*

"I'd like to frame this when we rebuild our lives," Nadia laughed, drawing a picture of a house.

"And I rent it, so that's easy for me. I'll just break the lease," she added, shrugging a shoulder.

"Damn, we are actually doing this," Dan happily said, leaning over and kissing Nadia passionately.

"I think I should go get changed. And maybe clean the blood up from my floor," Nadia said, standing up and stretching.

"Yeah, sorry about that. I'll help," Dan said, following her to the door, glad to see that Rupert was gone. Nadia opened her door and saw the dark smear across the wooden floors.

"It'll be easy, you go get dressed, I'll get started," Dan said, seeing Nadia becoming uncomfortable with the scene.

"Thanks," she whispered, heading into her bedroom, Dan getting to work right away. He pulled out bleach from her cleaning cupboard and decided to use his shirt as a rag to clean it up.

"It's not like I'll be needing this one

anymore," he happily said, mopping up the mess, his muscled body flexing as he did so.

"Huh, that was quick," he said out loud just as Nadia came back out of the room.

"Oh, wow. I had thought it would take longer. It always takes so long in the movies," she said, turning on the coffee machine.

"I was thinking. Maybe I don't want to own that bar. I think I'd like to live by the beach," Dan said, throwing his shirt in the bin.

"Yeah, same. I'll just do skype sessions with my therapist. Ever notice that therapist has a really unfortunate word in it? Let's go somewhere new," Nadia agreed, pouring sugar into her cup.

"I can't believe how much has changed in two hours," she laughed, sipping the drink.

"Yeah, right?" Dan agreed, shaking his head and sighing contentedly, closing his eyes and falling asleep, Nadia coming to join him, cuddling into him and falling asleep on his chest.

"Baby, wake up darling," Dan said, gently

rocking Nadia in his arms. The world had continued to spin around then while they had slept, the sun replaced by the moon the next time Dan had opened his eyes again.

"Huh?" Nadia asked, slowly blinking as she adjusted to the reality she now witnessed.

"What's the time?" She asked, laughing when she saw how dark the room was.

"8:30, we slept for the whole day," Dan said, his voice hoarse.

"Wow. Want to go to the movies?" Nadia asked, smiling in the dark, the moonlight which came through the windows outlining her form as she stood.

"Why not. It's not like we have to get up early in the morning," Dan said, cracking his back and yawning before turning on the light.

"Tomorrow I want to go to the real estate and sort out how to put my place on the market for tenants," he said, Nadia nodding her head.

"Ok, I'm just going to have a shower," Nadia said, walking to the bathroom, Dan following, wanting to see her body.

"Are you going just to stand there watching me?" She asked, Dan nodding, the toothy grin Nadia liked spreading across his face.

"Then put a song on," she instructed, causing Dan to raise his eyebrow.

"Please, Daddy," Nadia seductively added, waiting for the music to start.

"Um, probs not that one," she laughed as Dan played some metal song she had stopped liking years ago. Changing it to something more smooth, Dan gasped as he saw Nadia begin to dance.

"I had no idea you could move like that," he said, pulling the chair Nadia had in the corner over and sitting down.

"I've got a few tricks you're yet to learn of," she said, her hips rolling slowly, her eyes locking onto his, her hands moving over her body. She danced for Dan, enjoying how he looked at her like she held the answers to all his questions — sitting back down when she shook her head when he tried to come into the shower with her.

"I love you, Daddy," Nadia said, turning the water off and accepting the towel Dan passed her. Stopping the music, Dan just gulped.

"Please don't feel like you have to say that, I'm not going anywhere, you know that right?" He asked, drying Nadia's body.

"Do you really think I'd say it if I didn't mean it?" She whispered in his ear, giving him goosebumps.

"Alright, enough of that," he laughed, trying to get away from the closeness he felt his heart getting to Nadia's.

"No, stay here. Stay with me," she said, seeing the fear in his eyes.

"I'm not going to hurt you either," she added, looking up at him.

"I guess it has to go both ways, huh?" Dan said, trying to keep his heart open and connected to hers. Nadia nodded her head and refused to look away from him, a trick she had learned from her therapist, Dan matching her gaze with equal intensity.

"How did I get so lucky?" He asked, smiling vulnerably down on Nadia, feeling small and wondering if this is how Nadia felt all the time. Nadia just shrugged her shoulder, making him laugh and look at his watch.

"We will miss the movie if we don't get going," he said, Nadia, quickly running to the bedroom.

"What am I going to wear, Daddy?" Nadia called, waiting for him to come into the room.

"Let me see," Dan said, opening her cupboard and flicking through her clothes.

"These," Dan said, throwing a pair of black jeans on top of Nadia making her giggle.

"And this," he added, throwing her bra onto the bed next, followed by an old band t-shirt.

"Really?!" Nadia asked, getting covered in her black leather jacket with the black fur lining landing on her next.

"Yeah, what's wrong with that?" Dan asked, taking out her combat boots and pink socks from the top shelf and placing them down next to the bed.

"Nothing, now that I have my pink sockies," Nadia said, wiggling her toes into them as Dan helped her get dressed.

"Ok, now that you are all done, Daddy needs to get ready," Dan said, taking her hand and leading her out of her apartment and into his.

"I'll just be a moment," Dan said, as Nadia began to raid his fridge.

"We will get food out, bubba," he yelled from the bathroom hearing her open a packet of chips.

"That's fine, I'll eat these too though," she giggled to herself as she crunched on the potato chips.

They walked out onto the street 30 minutes later, hand in hand, feeling as though they had finally solved all their problems. Smiling up at Dan, Nadia squeezed his hand tighter in happiness, skipping along next to him. It was 10 o'clock, and Nadia loved how they took the back streets to the cinema. The full moon lit their path, and Dan stood taller than everyone who passed them, making Nadia feel safe and protected. They ordered tapas at the cinema restaurant and popcorn and ice cream when they bought their tickets before walking into the dark theatre. Sitting down quickly, Dan passed Nadia her popcorn and laughed as she became instantly perplexed on the big screen, kissing her on her forehead as she munched on the salty snack.

"This is a really good movie," Nadia tried to whisper but speaking in a loud hissing instead making Dan laugh.

"Shh, baby," he replied, settling into the seat and watching the film.

"Oh, you look sleepy, little one," Dan said as they exited the cinema. It was past midnight, and seeing Nadia clutch his arm nervously being out so late, he waited by the lights of the cinema entrance for a taxi, hailing for it as he saw the yellow vehicle approach. Giving the driver directions to his apartment, Dan wrapped his arm around Nadia who rested her head on his chest, closing her eyes and feeling herself fall asleep and falling into a dream about the girl in the tree. The girl with the dirt on her knees and hands, her hair falling out of her ponytail and her denim overalls with the tear on the thigh.

"What are you doing here?" Nadia heard herself saying to the girl who just laughed. "What do you mean? I live here! Maybe I should ask you the same question? You haven't visited me in forever!" The girl dramatically replied before giggling and jumping from the branch she was sitting on to one which was higher up the tree.

"Wait!" Nadia called, desperately trying to climb the tree to find the place where the girl was now sitting, swinging her legs over the edge and looking curiously at Nadia who finally reached the branch.

"You didn't use to take so long to climb up here," the girl said. Nadia just rolled her eyes as she sat next to the girl and looked out over the cityscape that greeted her eyes.

"As you said, it's been a while," Nadia said, taking in the view.

"Did you forget about me?" The girl said, having never taken her eyes off Nadia.

"What? No. Of course not, why would you say that?" Nadia angrily said, looking down at the girl who just raised an eyebrow at her.

"Yeah, you did. Just own it. You forgot about me. And now the question is, what are you going to do about it?" She challenged making Nadia scoff and look back out over the city. She saw the lights of the street flicker. She saw the red and white lights of the cars on the roads moving around the city like blood in its veins. She saw how Dan walked out of the apartment, and she saw herself run into his arms. Smiling, Nadia watched like a movie how they walked up their street, her heart full and saw how he passed her the lead of a big dog with a thick fluffy coat of black fur.

"Looks like you have everything you ever

wanted," the girl in the tree said, reaching out to place her hand over Nadia's.

"Yeah. So why do I still feel like this?" Nadia said, looking at the girl with tears in her eyes. The girl just took an envelope from her overall pocket. A drawing on ripped paper, the pieces having been taped together.

"You've never let me see this before," Nadia said, looking at the drawing she held in her hands. The picture she had ripped up herself when she had given it to her Father only to have him cruelly laugh at it and let it drop to the floor before walking out of the room.

"You did a good job of this actually. I really like how you made the sun so bright," Nadia said.

"He was really just such a jerk not to like it. Look at how pretty you made the house," Nadia said, repositioning herself as the girl sat on her lap.

"Really?" The girl asked, snuggling into Nadia. Nadia wrapped her arms around the girl and kissed her forehead as the girl began to cry.

"I won't forget about you again. I'm sorry I

did," Nadia whispered, the girl sucking her thumb as she just nodded her head and curled into Nadia.

"I've got you. You're alright," Nadia said, as she woke up, realizing that she was sucking her thumb, her cheeks wet with tears.

"You were crying in your sleep, baby," Dan said, his face full of concern. The taxi driver was collecting the change to give to Dan, and Nadia closed her eyes, wanting to be back in the tree, but the dream was gone.

"Yeah, fine," Nadia said as she got out of the taxi and made her way up the front steps of their apartment.

Chapter 9

"Are you going to tell me what you were dreaming about?" Dan asked as they entered his apartment. Nadia was tired, more psychologically than anything else and she just frowned at Dan who put both his hands up in defense.

"Or it can wait till morning," he quickly added, getting a faint smile from Nadia who dropped onto the couch.

"Oh no, baby girl, come on, don't fall asleep there," he said, walking over to her and picking her up before carrying her to the bedroom. Placing her down gently, he took her clothes off, receiving zero assistance from Nadia who closed her eyes and smiled as she felt Dan pull the sheets back and wrap her in her favorite pink blankets.

"Daddy," Nadia said, reaching for him, opening her eyes when she couldn't find him.

"Where are you?" She asked, wriggling out the warm cocoon Dan had settled her in and walking to the sound of Dan in the kitchen.

"I should have known you wouldn't have stayed where I left you. I'm just getting something to eat," Dan said, making a sandwich, offering Nadia bite, secretly glad when she declined.

"What are we even doing? We haven't even had a conversation about any of this, not really. We just kept coming up with ideas that we both liked that sound of," Nadia said, walking back to the bedroom with Dan. Going to the bathroom to clean their teeth before snuggling back in bed, Dan making Nadia her cocoon once more.

"Ok, let's have a conversation in the morning, little one," Dan said already half asleep. The nap Nadia had in the back of the taxi had done her wonders as she opened the window next to her side of the bed and counted the few stars that managed to shine out against the lights which light up the city. Letting her mind wander, she slipped into the memory of her dream. Nadia remembered wearing those overalls, how the dirt had gotten on her knees when she played football with the boys — tackling the boy who ran off and cried to his Mama because she got the ball off him.

"Loser," she said out loud thinking about him, the same smirk she had on her face then, re-emerging on her face in the darkroom she now lay in. She remembered how she had snuck into her teacher's art cupboard at school to steal the crayons she used to draw the picture for her Father. A girl in her class had caught her, which meant that Nadia had to confront her teacher. Nadia had straight-faced lied her ass off, following the only rule she ever listened to which was to deny till death. She'd been taught that one from her Father when the cops had come around to their house after someone had been shot on their front porch. She remembered the time she had slashed another teacher's tires when she had gotten in trouble, deciding that one wasn't enough.

"Fuck them all," she had said out loud as she dug the knife into the rubber, ripping the air out of them as though she was gutting a pig. Smiling, Nadia closed her eyes and turned into Dan, who opened his arms in his sleep and pulled her in close sighing happily in his sleep.

"Ok, let's do this properly," Dan said the next morning. He had set Nadia up in the corner of the living room, and she was busy coloring in a picture in the coloring in book he had bought her the previous week on his way home from work. He had gone into a toy store when the window display had caught his eye. The big pink and purple teddy bears on either side of the side large Ferris wheel in the middle of the window had candy in each of the carriages, but it was the blinking fairy lights that lined the bottom that sold him as he walked inside. Looking for both the pink and purple teddy bears, he bought those as well as a coloring in book that came with tubes of colored glitter. The glitter had been a hit, with Nadia using it for special pictures that Dan had proudly put on his fridge, after swearing black and blue that nothing would ever be put on there. He had one of the new model fridges that had a large touch screen on the front. Although he knew that he could take a photo of the adorable artworks that Nadia made for him, and display a photo of them on the screen, Dan loved the way Nadia's face had lit up when he had used sticky tape to secure the drawing. Dan was planning to take her shopping the next day to buy magnets, but he liked how rustic the tape looked.

"Ok, Daddy here is a list of things I've decided you need to do for me every day," Nadia said, giggling hysterically at her joke. Dan just chuckled as he walked over to where she was sitting and put her plate of star-shaped watermelon down in front of her, taking the coloring book away.

"Oh, thank you, Daddy," Nadia said, clapping her hands and opening her mouth. Dan placed a star in her mouth, and she ate happily while Dan read over her list. He laughed and took out her red crayon, and she instantly knew that her demands would not be met.

"No Daddy, they are non-negotiables," Nadia laughed, receiving another star.

"Getting extra treats because your teddies need treats too is non-negotiable?" Dan asked, making Nadia laughed as she rolled onto her back.

"Ok, let's be serious," Dan said, being serious, Nadia sitting up not wanting to annoy him.

"Ok," she said, still feeling little but being able to have this conversation.

"First of all, I already think we have a great handle on what you love and hate and I think that we have a really good balance of adult and baby time, what do you think?" Dan asked Nadia, nodding enthusiastically, and finishing her breakfast.

"I think the thing we need to discuss is, punishments," she said before hiding under her blanket.

"I don't ever want to punish you. What do you think our rules should be. You're already such a good girl, I can't imagine you doing something naughty," Dan said, making Nadia burst out laughing.

"You wait, I'm only perfect right now because I don't want to lose you," Nadia said giggling and coming out from under her blankie.

"Is that so?!" Dan asked, already knowing that it was the truth. Nodding, Nadia thought while Dan spoke.

"Ok, so rules. I'd like you to keep going for a run every second day, you always seem so happy when you go and so moody when you don't. You'll be Daddy's good girl at night, let me get you ready for bed, but during the day I'd like you to be a big girl unless I tell you otherwise. I still want you to call me Daddy and let me choose things for you like ordering at restaurants. And before you start to tell me no, don't worry I'll make sure I only order you things you actually like, I'm not mean!" Dan said when he saw Nadia put out that he wanted to order for her.

"Ok, but only the things I like," she said, making a point of this rule.

"Regarding punishments, what sort of thing

would you think suitable?" Dan asked, writing down notes as they spoke. Nadia thought, deciding that she'd enjoy spankings too much for them to be a punishment.

"I think something gross like, I have to eat only boiled vegetables for dinner, or I don't get an allowance for a week would be things I really didn't like. I'd just get turned on if you spanked me, Daddy," Nadia explained, Dan taking notes.

"So, if I bent you over my knee and pulled down your panties just to make your little ass red you'd find that hot?" Dan teased, grabbing at Nadia who giggled and playfully pushed him away, nodding her head and looking at him with innocent eyes.

"Noted," Dan said, stopping when he saw Nadia begin to regress. He cleared his throat and got up, taking her hand and pulling her to her feet.

"I think we have more than enough to go on sweetheart. How about we go for a drive, there is a really lovely place on the other side of town I'd love to take you too," Dan said, Nadia, following him to his room, sucking her thumb.

Nadia had been surprised that Dan wanted her to be his baby girl in public so quickly, and rolled around his bed as he diapered and dressed her. He had picked a puffy diaper, pink fluffy diaper cover and a white pinafore dress which made her breasts stand out. She had helped him by holding her feet still as he had put on her ankle socks and pink low-cut Converse sneakers before he took her hair out and placed a pink, glitter headband with a bow in her hair.

"Beautiful," he said, lifting her skirt and feeling the soft material of her diaper cover, making her giggle and push his hands away.

"Daddy, you're so silly," she said, blushing and turning away from him.

"One more thing," he said, taking out a pink pacifier and placing it in her mouth, exciting Nadia as she happily sucked on the big rubber nipple. Dan kissed her forehead, and he went to get dressed, coming back, and making Nadia's eyes go wide.

"You're pretty Daddy," she said when she saw his dark denim jeans, white long sleeve pullover and camel-colored cable knit cardigan with the sleeve rolled up. He smiled before scooping Nadia up and carrying to his car, happy that he wasn't as work as he buckled her into the passenger seat.

"Where are we going, Daddy?" Nadia asked as they drove out onto the road. Dan's big SVU roared into life as hit on the acceleration pedal, making Nadia laugh.

"There's this place that I heard about which is like a café designed for people in the community. I thought it might be nice to check it out together. Would you be interested in that? We can always go somewhere else if you aren't," Dan said but knowing Nadia's answer by the excitement in her eyes.

"Oh my god, yes please, Daddy. Let's go there," Nadia said, clapping her hands. She looked out the window and watched as they headed out of town and into a more suburban setting, confirming the belief Nadia held that the quiet streets in tree-lined suburbs were where all the really kinky people lived.

"We are almost there little one. If I'm wrong and this place sucks, we can leave straight away," Dan said, taking Nadia's hand in his as he drove off-road and down what looked like forest on either side of them.

"This is kinda scary," Nadia said, taking her pacifier out and looking out of the windows as they were suddenly driving on a black stone-paved road. Dan and Nadia both gasped at what they saw as the trees faded and what resembled a town emerged. In the middle of the dense forest which surrounded the property, what resembled a town had been built. There was a main street with middle-street parking, shops on either side. A toy store, multiple cafés, and restaurants, an ice cream shop, and bar and lounge were all on one side of the street, and as Dan made a U-turn to drive down the other side, Nadia turned to look at him in astonishment.

"Daddy, what is this place?!" She exclaimed as she saw the picnic area with the adult baby play equipment.

"I can't believe it either. I guess it's more than just a café. Let's park and go check it out," Dan said. As they drove to find a park, they both watched the people who moved about the street. Daddies and Mommies of all different styles looked after their littles, and she reached for Dan's hand.

"Who would work in these stores?" Nadia said to Dan, who unbuckled his seat belt. Getting out the car and coming around to her side, he undid her belt and took her from the truck.

"I guess people in the community, baby girl," Dan replied, still looking around in a daze. It was one thing to create a play space in their apartments, but this was public, open, a space where he could apparently bend Nadia over his knee and spank her ass without anyone batting an eyelid, as he saw a Mommy doing to her naughty boy.

"Are you still hungry? Let's go get some lunch," Dan said, pulling on Nadia's hand slightly as he walked with her to the closest restaurant. Going inside, he was just as surprised as he had been before with the sights which greeted him. There, Mommies were breastfeeding their littles, and littles colored in at the table while their Daddies talked and joked over steak sandwiches and beer. Caregivers spoon-feeding their babies or holding a bottle to their lips while they waited for their meal to be made, made Dan wonder how he had never heard of this whole place before. He took Nadia to one of the tables by the front window and sat down.

"This might be my favorite place in the whole world, Daddy!" Nadia exclaimed in a hushed squeal.

"I love it too," he replied as a mid-twenty-year-old woman approached the table.

"Hey, is it your first time here or do you know how our ordering system works?" She warmly asked.

"It's our first time," Dan replied, accepting the menus the woman gave him.

"Ok so, you can order from the menu directly. Or you can go over there and get the chief to create whatever you'd like from the fresh, locally sourced ingredients," the bubbly woman said. Nadia wondered how this place advertised for staff, deciding that she didn't care when the woman placed a coloring in book and crayons down in front of her.

"Cute bow, little one," she said before leaving the table to allow Dan and Nadia time to decide.

"Favorite place. This is it. This is my favorite place. I'm never leaving," Nadia said as she held up the packet of crayons for Dan to open.

Chapter 10

Dan, inspired by the hearty steak sandwich he saw others eating ordered one as well and for Nadia, he had ordered the fish and chips delighting her as the fish came out in fish shapes.

"Daddy this day is amazing," she said as he broke a piece of his burger off and let her try it.

"It's too spicy," she said, reaching for her sippy cup which Dan had placed on the table.

"I love that we don't have to be discrete here," he said as she sipped feverously.

After lunch, Dan held Nadia's hand as they walked down the street, smiling at the other people they met and Nadia beaming when she was complimented on how stunning her was in her outfit.

"I'm so pretty, Daddy, everyone thinks so," she gloated, making him laugh and roll his eyes.

"If we go into the toy store, you can only get one thing, alright? And only for $100 or less," Dan said, adding a price limit, knowing that Nadia would try to find the most expensive toy in the whole store if she could only have one. Snickering, Nadia knew why she was given a limit and wrapping her arms around Dan's, and she looked up at him with the big eyes he had first been captivated by.

"Thank you, Daddy," Nadia said, kissing his arm as he opened the door for her before they walked inside. As Nadia walked in, bubbles fell from the ceiling as the sensor set a bubble machine off delighting her and making her laugh as Dan waved them out of his way.

"Daddy, you're not meant to pop them!" Nadia happily giggled as she walked back over to Dan and took his hand, laughing as a bubble landed on her nose.

"Let's go over there," Dan suggested seeing the giant stuffies in the third row. Nadia was overcome with wonder as she looked up and down the shelves. Teddy bears, puppies, bunnies and kittens greeted her as she looked through the colors. Dan smiled and looked around, hoping there would be a chair, smirking when he saw another man sitting on a long lounge.

"Hey," Dan said, sitting down, giving the man a bro nod.

"Hi man. Get comfy, you'll be here a while if your little one is anything like mine," the man laughed.

"I'm Jeff," the man said, extending his hand.

"Dan," he replied, shaking Jeff's hand.

"First time?" Jeff asked, watching as Dan looked around at the customers in the store. He saw littles holding their caregiver's hands dressed in their little clothes and sucking on pacifiers. He saw a middle who was giving her Mommy attitude because she didn't want to leave the store without a spy toy she was clutching onto and he saw a little boy holding his Daddy's hand outside the store while his Daddy spoke on the phone.

"Is it that obvious?" Dan laughed as Nadia

came back with a large blue puppy stuffie.

"Daddy, may I please have this one?" Nadai asked, sitting on Dan's lap.

"Of course. Do you want to buy him yourself?" Dan asked, passing Nadia a $50 note. Nodding her head, she took the note and walked off to the counter.

"Sweet girl you've got there," Jeff said.

"Yeah, she's a keeper," Dan said, standing up and going to stand behind Nadia who was now being served by the cashier. Placing the puppy into Nadia's waiting arms, the cashier smiled at her as they left the store.

"I think I will name her, Starfish," Nadia giggled. Dan loved it when she was in one of her happy, silly moods and rolled his eyes at her dramatically.

"Starfish?" He questioned, only making Nadia continue to giggle.

"Yep. That's her name Daddy, Starfish," Nadia said, deciding that her joke was in fact now the toys serious name. Dan just laughed as he led her back to where the truck was parked.

"Time to go baby girl. I bet you are tired after such a big day," Dan said, ignoring Nadia who shook her head no as he buckled her into the front seat and placed her paci in her mouth, pulling her seat back until she was almost laying down.

"Shut your eyes little one, I know you're sleepy," Dan said, placing his hand on her tummy and patting her gently as he drove out of the street, back down the long road and out onto the street of the 'real world.' It felt as though he had been in a dream as he drove back to their apartment. The people in their adult clothes, the busy lives they seemed to be living. He had almost forgotten the feeling of stress, and as he saw people angrily talking into their phones. He looked over at Nadia, her eyes closed and her lips slightly pushed out around the pacifier in her mouth and sighed.

I don't know how life gets any better than this, he thought to himself.

"Daddy, do you think we should get a puppy?" Nadia said three weeks later. Since going to 'little world' which is what Nadia had taken to affectionately calling it, Nadia had become obsessed with puppies.

"A puppy?!" Dan said, almost choking on the cereal he was eating. Nadia just looked at him plainly as she nodded her head, fully expecting that her request would be granted. That had been the pattern she had come to know as true. All she had to do was continue to please Dan, following his rules, completing the tasks he had set for her, and she would be rewarded with whatever her heart desired.

"I don't know sweetie," he said, making her mind confused.

"What do you mean, Daddy?" She asked, trying not to sound disappointed. Dan put the newspaper he was reading down and looked at her. Her innocent face looking ever so slightly annoyed.

"Well, a puppy doesn't stay a puppy. It

turns into a dog, and dogs live for a very long time. What happens if you decide you want to up and go somewhere? What happens to the dog if we can't find a place which lets us move in with a dog?" Dan asked, folding the newspaper and looking directly at Nadia who had a serious look on her face.

"These are all good points, but, Daddy, I think you are missing something," Nadia said, putting her crayons down to match the attention Dan was putting on the topic.

"Which is?" He asked, slightly amused. This is what Dan loved about having Nadia as his little. She was polite and obedient, and she knew how to word her arguments in a way that wasn't bratty or irritating.

"We would move into a pet-friendly place first and then get the dog. We would only go on adventures which we could take the dog on, and anyway, you said you love camping, and you can always take a puppy on camping trips," Nadia explained, happy that Dan hadn't shut her idea down completely.

"I'll think about it," he said. Dan's answer translated in Nadia's mind as 'I need more convincing,' so she immediately got busy on her puppy marketing strategies as she found a blank piece of paper and began drawing puppies.

"What Daddy? It's the law of attraction," Nadia giggled, the mischief in her eyes entertaining Dan as he watched her, her cheeky grin unable to hide her delight in playing in the grey zone of their dynamic.

"We could take her to 'little world,'" Nadia casually said as she colored, Dan sipping his coffee and looking at her over the edge of his cup.

"Ok, what would you call her then?" Dan said, entertaining the idea. Nadia thought for a moment before taking out a blank piece of paper and scribbling down what looked like a list of names. Dan peered over the table to get a closer look and read the names Nadia was considering out loud.

"Evie, Scarlet, Harriet," Dan read, pausing at the last name.

"Harriet? Have you ever heard of a dog called Harriet?!" He said as his laughter escaped and caused Nadia to look at him with those playful eyes, he adored so much.

"Daddy!" She exclaimed, surprised that he would make fun of her choices.

"Ok, what else have you got. We are not having a dog called, Harriet," Dan laughed, rolling his eyes.

"Suddenly that's my favorite name," Nadia said looking at him with a slight challenge in her smirk.

"Like it all you want, it's not happening," Dan said, making his intention clear.

"What about Cupcake?" Nadia said, laughing as she tilted her head back.

"Alright, alright. Evie. What about Evie?" She suddenly said, realizing that Dan was not the least bit amused.

"Evie will do fine," he said, getting up to kiss her forehead.

"But I never said we are getting a dog, just

that I wanted to know what name you'd give it," Dan said, putting the dishes of their breakfast in the dishwasher.

"Mm-hmm," Nadia replied, knowing in her heart that it was only a matter of time before they got a dog.

"Hi, we'd like to look at the dogs. I don't really know how to say that any better, first time," Nadia said in her usual tactless manner making Dan smirk behind her. It had taken him less than a week to take her to the pound. She put it down to her silent protesting of puppy pictures and only wanting to hear stories about dogs as she fell asleep at night. Dan knew that they were only there because he couldn't see why he'd make her wait for a dog when it would hardly cause a dint in their lives, but he let Nadia think it was all her.

"Ok, head out back, and if you see one you like, you'll need to come back and fill out the paperwork and pay the fee," the lady at the counter said as she opened the back door which led to the barking dogs in kennels that made Nadia cringe.

"I'm not a fan," Nadia whispered to Dan as she looked around the sad faces of the dogs that starred back at her.

"Yeah, rough," Dan replied, bending down to look at a massive pitbull, the dogs eyes cautious of him. Dan stood back up and looked at Nadia, taking her hand in his.

"Maybe we've made a mistake," he said frowning.

"No. We haven't. We might just need to rethink," Nadia said which instantly made Dan nervous. Whenever Nadia had a thought that made her eyes glitter the way they did right now, he knew that they were in for an adventure.

"There's only four dogs in here. Let's get them all," Nadia said, Dan, closing his eyes and taking a breath.

"How are we suppose to choose just one?!" Nadia said, her heartbreaking as she saw the sad faces of the dogs. Dan opened his eyes and looked down at her, biting his bottom lip.

"Baby," Dan started to say, still deep in thought. Nadia just looked back at eyes that he knew he could hardly say no too.

"Look, little one. We simply don't have the space to put them. We can't look after four dogs," he said gently but seeing the unwavering reserve on Nadia's face.

"We can just buy a small house on a big bit of land out west," Nadia replied. This was another thing Dan loved about her. She had that, childlike hope that everything can be fixed. She didn't live in a world with constraints. She lived in a world where anything and everything was possible. He smiled, asking himself why he was acting like such an adult when his own spirit wanted to be as free as hers and just laughed as he nodded. His eyes looking into hers, her innocence beaming from them and her hero being him.

"I guess I better get that apartment of ours on the market for sale and not tenants hey, little one?" He said, smiling as she skipped next to him

as they went back out to the front counter and buy
all four dogs.

Chapter 11

"This is the coolest thing I've ever done!" Nadia said on the drive home. In the back seat of Dan's truck sat the massive Pitbull he had seen first which Nadia had called Evie, two Staffordshire Bull Terriers call Henry and Sasha, and a white Bull Arab Dan named Venus. Nadia watched how they rested against each other, accepting pats from her as she reached behind into the back seat.

"Baby, turn back around," Dan said as they drove through the city. They were on their way to the pet store, Dan explaining that he would go in and buy the basics but that they could go together to the store again once their new family was set up to buy special things for each of their new fur babies. Nadia had giggled happily, placing her feet on the edge of the seat and holding her knees together.

"I'll go to the real estate tomorrow to sort out the house situation. I want you to look for houses with a large patch of land, somewhere in the country I think, little one," Dan explained as he pulled into the pet parking lot and kept the air con running.

"Lock the doors when I get out sweetie," he said, kissing her on the forehead and patting the dogs before leaving the truck. Nadia took out her phone and quickly got to work, searching for property all over the state, hoping to find something suitable. It hadn't escaped her that they were living a life, not many of their friends or family understood. They would understand it even less once they learned of the new additions to the family and their potential new home. Nadia wondered when she had become so fearless, so free and so willing to explore all the possibilities the world presented. She flicked through the search, marking several properties that fit their budget and noted that they would really be making the country switch.

"How did you go?" Dan suddenly said opening the door after having put four dog begs, four collars and leashes, dog bowls, toys and two huge bags of dry food in the tray of the truck.

"So good. Oh my gosh, I hope you like them. I think this could be really fun," Nadia said, watching as Dan looked intently at a farm ranch two hours away.

"This one. Let's put an offer on it today. I can just see you plucking the flowers around this big old tree here in the middle of the yard and putting them in your hair, the pups running around happily. Baby, thank you for making my life so fun, it's sure as hell never boring with you," Dan said, handing her back the phone and driving out onto the road. He turned the radio up, rolled the windows down, and laughed how the dogs stuck their heads out of the windows wanting to feel as free as he and Nadia craved.

"This is living," he whispered, looking over at Nadia who let the wind sweep her hair, watching the people walk out of their office buildings, seeing their drained faces, wondering how he could have ever thought that that life was worth living.

They arrived home and took the dogs inside, setting up their beds in the living room and food bowls on the balcony outside.

"I'm pretty sure that we can't have animals in this building, even though you own it, Daddy," Nadia said, playing with the rope he had bought for the dogs.

"Shh, I won't tell if you don't," Dan said in a hushed tone, the look in his eye telling her everything she needed to know.

"I think you've been a big girl for about as long as I think you can stand. Come to Daddy little one, let me look after you," Dan said, not having to repeat himself as Nadia jumped into his arms and snuggled into his neck.

"Oh, I hadn't realized you were so close to being my sweet angel again. Did Daddy get you just in time?" Dan asked Nadia, putting her thumb in her mouth just to have Dan replace it with a pacifier. Nadia closed her eyes as he walked her to the bathroom, knowing that the dogs would be happy playing in the living room for a moment. He placed her down on the ground and closed the door behind them, taking of her adult clothes and putting them in the wash basket, turning the bath on and letting the tub fill with sweet-smelling bubbles before picking her up and lowering her into the warm water.

"Duckie?" Dan asked, seeing Nadia close her eyes and curl up into the fetal position.

"No thanks, Daddy," she replied, breathing deeply. She wasn't sure why she felt like this after being out of the house for hours at a time. It was almost as though she was a sponge and had absorbed too much water, not being able to take anymore, and shutting down was her only coping strategy that made sense. She felt her heart pounding as though she was having a panic attack, her head spinning with images and flashing lights she couldn't slow down.

"It's alright sweetie, just breathe, I've got you," Dan softly said, seeing her try to unwind in front of him.

"It hurts, Daddy," Nadia said softly.

"I know darling, just breathe. You're alright, you're safe, nothing bad is going to happen to you," he said, stroking her hair and gently washing her toned body. He had seen her go through this before and was glad that he finally knew how to help her. He turned the lights off, opened the shutters on the windows, and let the moonlight stream into the room — the neon lights reflecting on the ceiling. Nadia sighed, opened her eyes and breathed as though she had just ran up a hill as she tried to calm herself.

"Thanks, Dada," she said, whatever this feeling was, wash over her, and her heart returning to beating regularly.

"That was quick this time. I'm proud of you. I still think that it is post-traumatic stress baby," Dan said, taking a towel from the rail and help Nadia out of the bathtub.

"I don't know. I have another therapy session this week. I'll probs go and have to guess what is troubling me again," Nadia replied, discontent in her voice which just made Dan laugh.

"Then go to another therapist?" He suggested making Nadia shake her head.

"No I like her, she just makes me have to do the work and I'd much rather she just tell me what's wrong with me," she explained. Dan finished drying her off and took her hand as he opened the door to find the four dogs laying contently in the hallway, getting up as they saw the door open.

"Hi guys," Dan said, happy with their decision to buy all four dogs.

"So she helps stand you up but makes you take the steps on your own two little feet," he teased making Nadia laugh.

"I guess so," she yawned, stretching her body and arching it until she felt like it would snap before relaxing on the bed and watching as the dogs found a new spot on the floor. Dan went to the cupboard and took out a diaper, long-sleeved purple onesie, and black thigh high socks.

"Stay still for Daddy," Dan said, adding double thickness to the diaper before quickly fastening it around her waist.

"Daddy, I don't like it," Nadia said, squirming on the bed, feeling too big to be diapered so heavily.

"That's ok," Dan said, holding Nadia's ankles down and forcing her socks on.

"Don't be naughty for Daddy or you'll feel my hand on your pretty little ass," Dan growled making Nadia tense her calves. He had never had to punish her before, and she really wasn't interested in it happening tonight. She lay still and let Dan pull the onesie tight over her diaper and push the material into her pussy. Rubbing over her body, Dan smiled in satisfaction, patting her predatorily.

"There's my good girl," he said, reaching for her and lifting her effortlessly into his arms, carrying her back out into the living room and placing her down on the couch. Going into the kitchen, he took out steak and vegetables, beginning to cook as Nadia watched cartoons and played with the dogs.

Chapter 12

The apartment sold faster than Dan or Nadia had expected, and within a month they were needing to move out and into a new place. Having had no luck with buying a property, they decided to widen their search and had found an old farmhouse on a large property in a town that neither of them had ever heard the name before.

"What if it sucks?" Nadia said, driving through the town and looking back to check on the dogs. They looked back at her, their happy faces making her whole being feel alive. Dan had had custom made dog cages built, with the air-con system integrated so they would always be comfortable, depending on the weather. Nadia loved that Dan was so thoughtful like that.

"Well, I guess we won't get it," he laughed back, wondering why she would think they'd buy something which didn't suit them.

"Yeah I know, but we are running out of time, and I just think that maybe, we might need to like, renovate it something and that might be a good thing to keep in the back of our minds," Nadia explained. Dan looked at her, a sideward smirk spreading across his lips. He winked at her, reaching over to hold her hand, bringing it up to kiss it and squeezing it gently but excitedly.

"Ok. Don't worry, darling. I won't let us be homeless," Dan said, reading her mind even when she didn't want him to. Nadia just rested her head against the headrest and looked at him, tracing her fingers over his defined jawline, making him smile as he drove up the dirt driveway.

"I think we are here, little one," Dan said, peering out through the windscreen. Nadia raised an eyebrow.

"Time to play the big girl game," she laughed, making Dan smirk as they both got out of the truck, Dan greeting the agent who was waiting for them.

"The property is ready to go, all you'd have to do move your furniture in, it really is such a steal especially in this current market," the real estate man. Dan knew that he knew him from somewhere and missed all the things he was telling them as he racked his brain, trying to figure out where he had seen him before. The man took them through the farmhouse, Nadia falling in love with it instantly. The bones of the house were solid, and she could picture how the new kitchen and bathroom would look, how the rooms would be made fresh with a bit of paint, but when she looked over at Dan, his mind was clearly elsewhere.

"What do you think?" The real estate man asked both of them. Nadia looked at Dan, who was still trying to figure out where he knew this man from.

"I think I'd like to take a look around the yard with the dogs," Nadia said, wanting to get Dan away and to herself to ask him what the hell he was doing. The man nodded, going into the spare room as he waited for Nadia and Dan to be finished with their inspection.

"What are you doing?" Nadia asked Dan as they opened the dogs' cages.

"I think I know him from somewhere," Dan said, taking Sasha down and letting her run after the other three as Nadia turned to look at him with disbelief.

"What?" He asked, curious as to why she had a problem.

"Daddy, have you even seen the house?" She asked, sighing and leaning against the truck.

"Yeah. I like it. What about you? Shall we put an offer on it?" He said, Nadia, rolling her eyes but nodding her head.

"That's it!" Dan suddenly said, Nadia, not amused one bit.

"He was the guy I met the first time we went to 'little world!' We were in the toy store. I sat down next to him," Dan said, feeling highly accomplished.

"That's great, Daddy," Nadia said, unsure

about what this had to do with anything.

"I think we should put an offer in right now. Let's go do that," Dan said, whistling to the dogs who began to run back to them.

Dan and Nadia drove home after getting their offer accepted and signing papers, the nights' sky covering the windscreen.

"Daddy, I think your tummy is telling me that it wants to get take out," Nadia said, trying to sound as serious as she could but letting a small giggle escape.

"I think it's more your tummy than mine," Dan teased back checking the time.

"It is late, yeah fuck it, good call," Dan said, pulling into the first burger joint he found.

"Lol, yeah fuck it," Nadia replied, making Dan whip his head around at her in surprise.

"You know better than to swear like that little lady. I guess Daddy should have led by better example," Dan said, taking her out of the truck before putting the dogs on their leashes and tieing them to a post out the front.

"You want to stay with them for a minute. I know what you'll want. Double cheeseburger with a small fries and a large choc shake, extra sauce, no pickles," Dan said, making Nadia smile and tilt her head from side to side.

"Yep," she laughed.

Dan came back five minutes later, a tray in his hands and set it down on the table.

"Life is nice with you," he whispered in her ear and kissed her cheek, surprised when she turned her head and kissed him full on the lips.

"Woah," Dan said, pulling away, breaking the kiss and looking at Nadia with wide eyes.

"I want to, Dan," Nadia said, making Dan almost jump out of his seat with excitement. She had told him months ago that if he wanted to be with her, he'd have to wait a long, long time before he had her body in any kind of adult way. For the first time, she felt strong. She felt like sex wouldn't be something to force, something to fight. She wanted to know what it felt like to smile instead of frowning as she connected instead of being taken.

"I don't want you to think that just because we have this house now that you owe me or something," Dan said, making Nadia laugh.

"Don't flatter yourself," she said, rolling her eyes as her guard went back up. Taking a few mouthfuls of her burger before speaking again, he watched her with a curiosity that was never quenched.

"It's not like that. I am just ready, that's all," she softly said, the world fading all around them.

"So finish your fries. Coz I wanna ride your dick," Nadia whispered getting up and going to put her rubbish in the bin.

"Does this feel weird for you?" Dan said, unbuttoning his shirt in the moon light-filled room an hour later. Nadia just laughed and nodded her head.

"Like I've seen you naked heaps of times, you've seen me too, but this feels different," Dan said, kicking his shoes off.

"Different naked," Nadia agreed, swallowing hard.

"What are you into?" Dan suddenly asked, realizing that he had never asked her how she liked to fuck before. Nadia froze for a moment, unsure how to answer that question.

"I don't know. I honestly don't. I've done a heap of stuff, sure, but was I into it. I'm not sure," she replied, standing in front of Dan with just her panties on.

"Ok, wanna try, like, everything then?" Dan said as if they had nothing to lose. Nadia just nodded and shrugged as she looked around the room nervously.

"This is dumb, why are we so nervous," she said, wanting to feel anything except for the feeling of vulnerability.

"I'm not nervous; you are," Dan laughed, surprised that his palms were getting sweaty.

Gross, he thought, going over to the bed and wiping them on a pillow before throwing it on the floor.

"Do you want to do this in bed?" Nadia asked, seeing him sitting there, a dumb smile on his face.

"I guess, most people do at some point," he said, sighing and wishing he could shake the first time terrors he hadn't felt since high school.

"You got me feeling like a kid," Dan said, shaking his head.

"Welcome to my world," Nadia replied, making him laugh as she climbed into bed beside him.

"So. This is the story we are going to be telling? That we were both too scared actually to do anything, so we just made jokes all night?" Nadia said, laughing and looking down into her lap.

"I must say, it is really nice that we can make jokes thought," Dan said, Nadia, cutting him off by pressing her lips to his.

"Oh wow, we are really doing this," he muttered through the kiss.

"Yeah, we are," Nadia said, taking his hand

and placing it on her body, smiling into the kiss as she felt him take over. He pulled her into his body, laying side by side as his fingers ran through her hair and over her breasts, feeling his dick surge with enjoyment as he squeezed them.

"You're wet," Dan said, sounding surprised.

"That's usually taken as a good sign," Nadia said as she rolled him onto his back and placed her hand on his chest as she reached behind and jerked his dick making him involuntarily gasp. Nadia moved down and felt his hard cock against her slit, pausing for a moment. She looked at him, with his loving eyes that seemed to read into her soul. His mouth that had never uttered anything but kindness and admiration. His hands which had only ever held her in the highest regard, as she slowly allowed him to enter her with gentle ease. Biting her bottom lip and closing her eyes as she lifted off him just to grind down again, she smiled.

"You've got me," Dan softly said as he sat up and held her to his lap, bucking his hips forward, Nadia wrapping her arms around his neck. She rested her head on his shoulder, placing her hand over his heart, feeling his pulse as he continued to fill her. Panting, he lay back down, turning over with Nadia's instigation and kissed her forehead feeling his senses heighten with each thrust. Holding himself up over her, she felt his muscled arms pulsate and his back rippled with intention.

"Dan," Nadia whispered, lifting onto her elbows as she kissed him, exploring him with more eagerness. He rested on his forearm and ran his fingers through her hair, down her cheek and wrapped his hand behind her head, holding her to him.

"I'm right where I want to be," she said, taking both hands and holding his face still, looking into his eyes, he buckled and dropped his body onto hers making her laugh and groan at the sudden weight crushing her body.

"Way to kill the mood," he said, on shaky arms trying to reposition himself, stopping when Nadia shook her head no.

"It's ok. Come here," Nadia said, pulling him

back down on her smaller body. He rested his head against her neck, kissed along her collar bone and wrapped his arms around her.

"Well, I guess this is goodbye to my heart, it's yours now," Nadia said as she felt her orgasm begin to edge dangerously close.

"We can stop if you'd like," Dan said, never actually wanting to leave with bed with her. Nadia just shook her head as she took his hand and placed it on her ass, showing him how she wanted to be touched. Surprised, Dan slapped and groped at her fighting off his climax, desperate to cum with her instead.

"Oh, Nadia, god damn," he said, feeling her break, joining her immediately. She giggled as she felt him fill her, surprised that her usual reaction to want to go and have a shower, seemed to be non-existent with him. She lay there, in the bed with him, wrapped up in his arms and couldn't remember frowning once.

"That was different," she said, moving away from him and going to put a shirt on. Dan watched as she disappeared into the bathroom, only to see her come back a minute later. She was wearing the crimson lace panties he had seen her buy online but had never seen her wear and smiled at how her messy hair, white t-shirt, and sexy panties made him weak for her all over again.

"You really are the most beautiful woman I have ever seen, Nadia," Dan breathlessly said, feeling his heart beat for her in a way that it hadn't before tonight. She playfully posed for him, jumping back into bed and into his arms.

"Is this our life now? We have magical sex, live in the country with our big dogs? Don't have enter the rat race? I mean, I love it, but what are we going to do when the money runs out?" Nadia said, knowing that their work free bliss would not be able to be maintained forever. Dan deeply exhaled while he thought.

"Yeah, pretty much. I love magical sex with you, I've never felt so, I don't even know, powerful maybe? It's something more than strong, it's like I could be an air bender or something," Dan said, the bewilderment in his experience making Nadia smile to herself.

"Air bender? Ok, Mr Air bender. I think it might be like, alignment. Everything has gone from absolute chaos to peace, power, certainty, and balance," Nadia said, getting tickled as she teased Dan.

"I think that when we move into the town, we should look for jobs we can do online so that we can work to our own schedules. There are more jobs online than there is in the 'real world' so it might be a good move," Dan said, Nadia accepting immediately.

"Sounds good to me," she said, getting back up and holding her hand out to him.

"It's been fun, but I'm tired Daddy," Nadia said, instigating the return of their DDLG dynamic. Dan beamed and jumped into action, turning on the light and near blinding both of them.

"Daddy!" Nadia exclaimed as she covered her eyes but feeling Dan take her hand.

"Here I am," he said leading her to the

bathroom and running a shower for the both of them. Soaping her body with the strawberry body wash she loved so much, she made bubbles with it, happy when Dan didn't pop them. Getting out, Dan knew how tired Nadia was by how quiet she had become and smiled lovingly at her. He dipped his head to see her eyes were closed while he dried her.

"Not much longer, baby girl," he said picking her up and taking her back to the bedroom. Ripping the sheets off the bed and quickly putting on new ones, before Dan lay Nadia down, he placed her matte black pacifier in her mouth and watched as she fell asleep almost instantly. Laughing to himself, he secured a diaper to her and gently dressed her in her favorite crimson long-sleeved onesie, making sure to push up the sleeves and tucked her up in bed. Dressing himself in long grey sweatpants, he joined her and cradled her in his arm, pressing her against his body. He organized how they move all their belongings to the new house while she slept soundly against his chest.

Chapter 13

"Nadia, are you ever going to tell me what is it that keeps you up at night?" Dan said, suddenly over dinner three months later. They had successfully made the old farmhouse into a home they could both enjoy by repainting it and putting in a new kitchen and bathroom. The dogs were playing in the yard, and Nadia watched as they chased each other over logs and through the trees.

"I know that he just up and left one day, but there's more. I can see it little one, and I want to help you with it," Dan said, reaching out to hold her hand making her flinch and look at him before biting her bottom lip.

"Why do you even care. Most guys don't want to hear about the ex that still manages to ruin a perfect day," Nadia said, making Dan smirk.

"I'm not like most guys," he replied without

missing a beat.

He has a point., she thought, shrugging her shoulders.

"Alright, here is it," she said, taking a deep breath and exhaling before looking at him.

"He called out, *it's dinner time,* as he washed his hands before coming back over to me. I was failing at trying not to be pouty," Nadia began to explain.

"He said, *I warned you what would happen if you weren't good for me, and now you're sulking?* I just looked at him angrily and shaking my head no," Nadia said, getting up and moving to sit on Dan's lap.

"*No? You're not bratty? Because this is not what not being bratty looks like,* he whispered to me before I told him I didn't need such a thick diaper. I pulled my puppy dog eyes, the ones which had served me so well in the past, but it didn't work. I was shocked when I saw him flex his hips forward and unbuckle his belt. Doubling it over, I swallowed hard, my eyes going wide and tensing my calves," she continued, feeling Dan's arms wrap around her waist.

"Get over my lap; he had calmly said, which just made me more nervous. I slowly obeyed, hoping that he wasn't going to go hard on me. Rubbing my ass, he placed his other hand on my throat and gently caressed my skin, feeling for my pulse, smiling as he felt it race." Nadia reached for her sippy cup, not wanting to remember what came next, the memory which still haunted her even on perfect days.

"Breath, he whispered almost lovingly, only adding to my confusion. He took his time running the belt over the exposed flesh of my thighs and laughed when body involuntarily shivered, goosebumps covering my skin," she said before biting her bottom lip, looking at Dan's gentle eyes for reassurance.

"Daddy, please don't, I softly begged, a tear escaped and fell onto the couch. *But how will you learn not to complain to me about your diaper if I don't sweetie?* He teased, continuing to trace my

body with the belt. Looping it around my neck and pulling it until he heard me choke. Wrapping the strap around his fist, he pulled, jerking my head back, forcing a breathless gasp to escape as my eyes began to water. *Does being a bad girl for Daddy still feel like a good idea?* He had whispered in my ear as his hand came down hard on my left thigh, making me bite my bottom lip and close my eyes." Nadia stood up and paced the room, unsure of how she had ever let herself be used so viciously.

"*No, Daddy,* I replied as another spank landed on my right thigh. I felt the sting burn on the softest parts of my body as he continued to spank me, making my legs go red, the skin rising. I knew that they were being to welt. I lost count and stopped wincing against the impact and simply allowed him to have me. My body fell limp on his lap. My head dipped as the leather belt crushed into my wipe pipe. Feeling my surrender, finally stopped and supported held my head as he loosened the belt and took it from my neck.

Placing it down next to him and turning me over, I guess he was surprised at how glassy eyes my eyes were. I just blankly stared at the ceiling." Nadia explained, sitting against the wall and getting covered by dog cuddles.

"*Baby?* He asked, clicking his fingers in front of my face, waiting for my eyes to focus on him, smiling at me when they slowly did. *Are you alright, darling? I'm sorry I had to do that, Daddy doesn't like having to punish you, but I will not let you be a brat,* he said, as my gaze looked back at him with emptiness. *Come on, let me remind you that you are the most special part of my life,* he said, picking me up and taking me into the bedroom, pulling the sheets down and lowering my limp body into bed. But I was done, there was nothing he could do to make up how far he had gone, nothing I could do to take back how silent I had fallen," she said, Dan getting up to make a cup of sweet tea. He hated stories like this, the ones where the people who are meant to look after someone simply, don't.

"Can you talk to me? He asked, getting slightly annoyed that I seemed to have lost my light, my sparkle. I just looked back at him, unsure of what I was meant to say. Closing my eyes, I turned around and away from him, only making him more annoyed. Reaching for my shoulder, he turned me back around, glaring into my face, but my eyes staring straight through him. *Nadia, don't be like this, you know that if you broke a rule, that this would be the punishment,* he said, only to be again greeted with my back once more as I turned over and let my tears silently fall onto the pillow as he sighed angrily and walked out of the room, shutting the door behind him," Nadia explained, wiping a tear that fell on her cheek as she got up and walked into the kitchen. Sitting up on the bench, she swung her legs on the bench as she sipped the tea Dan had made for both of them.

"I thought for days about it. I'd leave for work really early and get home way after the city had closed. I just kept thinking, Why didn't I just stop him? He never actually wanted to hurt me. He would have stopped. He would have fucking stopped. But I just didn't think about it at the time. I was so obsessed with doing what I was told, hoping that I'd be given the smallest of kindnesses after," Nadia continued, shrugging her shoulders as Dan stood in front of her and placed his hands on her thighs.

"Did you ever have a conversation with him about what had gone down?" Dan asked. Nadia loved that this was his first reaction to communicate. She had been surprised at how solution based he was when they had first gotten together, but now it just made her heart dance, that in the midst of his anger, he would always stop and redirect the discussion towards a solution.

"Kinda, I told him, *it was really not cool what I let you do. I'm not down for that kind of impact, you gave me fucking nothing afterward, and I really don't trust you anymore. I'm coming home to talk about this with you. I should have said red. I take full responsibility for that. But I also think you shouldn't have been such a dickhead when you didn't get your way.* He tried to be playful, but I just shook my head and said, *Don't. There's like zero dynamic here right now. I'm trying to fix this. I'm trying to stay when all I want to do is run away and smash in all the windows on your truck.* He didn't think that was as endearing as I had tried to make it sound," Nadia explained making Dan laugh. He picked her up and took her to the couch, sitting her in her blanket nest and cuddling her as she continued to share her story.

"He goes, *I know I fucked up. I shouldn't have gone so hard on you. You did break a rule though,* and I said, *I broke a rule yes, I didn't deserve to be pushed that far. I can accept that I didn't look after myself, but I thought I could trust you and if you can't even take responsibility for your part then, what the fuck are we even doing here?* He couldn't answer me so I just rolled my eyes and said, *well, that's that then,* and I just turned and walked away out of the apartment, as I decided he could keep my clothes," Nadia said to a speechless Dan.

Dan sat at the table in silence, surprised that Nadia had been so badly treated by someone who was meant to be the one person in the world that wouldn't hurt her. Silently grateful that it hadn't worked out with anyone else so that he could have her all to himself.

"I'm so sorry that happened to you. How sick and twisted, as if he couldn't see he had pushed you past your limit, no one is that stupid," Dan said, leaning over and kissing her forehead.

"It doesn't matter," Nadia began to say, getting cut off by Dan who placed his finger to her lips.

"Don't say that. It does matter, or you wouldn't still be broken by it," he corrected, making her resent that he was right but love that he knew her well enough to be able to call her out on it.

"Come on, you've told me, but you should write about it," Dan said, getting up and opening the back door, a gush of cold air flooding the house making Nadia's heart dance.

"See? The night is calling you, come on. I'll get some candles and whiskey, and the dogs can play. Maybe I'll light a little fire, and we can roast marshmallows," he said, walking around the house collecting the things they would need for their impromptu evening under the stars.

Nadia stayed out as the night grew late, Dan coming out to light some candles and sip whiskey as she wrote on her laptop.

I did it. I survived it all. I knew I'd find happy one day and that one day finally happened. I got to the top, I finished the race, and now I'm looking around, and all I know is that now that I'm at the top, I won't let anything or anyone hurt that precious little one who still lives inside of me. Ain't no one going to take her hand and pull her down again. I used to think that strength was hard and cold and angry, but it isn't. It's something between peace and crying, somewhere in the middle of a heart that beats a pace to fast and eyes that let tears fall. It's a place next to hell and sorry, and I guess I'll do better next time. Kinda like when the sky breaks with blinding sunlight that's almost trying to burn your eyes out but helping you too clearly see after an overcast day. I don't know when I decided that I needed to become myself. Maybe it had just become too heavy carrying this sack of shit around. Maybe it was when I felt sick to my stomach every time I was hugged. It was probably when I couldn't breathe without feeling like it was still happening. I sure did give them more than I'd taken, I was too hard on myself, and I was broken and didn't know how to ask for help. I just allowed it to carve out some awful version of who I could be and in its wake, let go of everything good and true and real. Healing hasn't been what I thought it'd be. It's more like going ten rounds with the bruising only coming through in the morning. The real pain starts a few days later when you can hardly get your heavy heart out of bed, the weight of it needing to be carried with two hands when you are alone.

Too bad that you're going into battle for the next five days, too bad that you can hardly breathe your tears back, too bad that you can't bleed for them when you are so busy being your own champion. Nadia took her hands from the keyboard and read her words out loud; the melody almost lyrics from a sad country song. She looked at the tumbler of whiskey sitting next to her laptop, the wooden table making the yellow liquid look darker as she swirled it in the crystal glass. Bring it to her lips, she breathed in the scent and let it burn her mouth before swallowing more than she could hold, spilling it from the side of her mouth as she gasped as it stripped her throat. Looking at Dan, curled up on the chair in the corner, a blanket over him and surrounded by dogs, she knew he would be asleep till morning. She knew that she had tonight. It was rare that she was awake when he was not and yet, it was in the stillness of the late of night that she found herself sitting there in the dark back porch, her laptop keyboard light and the nearly burnt out candles eliminating the space.

I wonder if anyone can feel me sitting here,

open, vulnerable, tipsy, and thinking about marrying him,* she considered, putting her earphones in and finding the songs which soothed her wild, torn heart.

I just need to get my money right, give him the ring he deserves, give him the proposal that will take his breath away, and make him cry. I wish I could do it now, take him to the place, have the ring made, scream from the bottom of heart, the depths of my soul, will you marry me? Maybe my heart needed to be torn open so I could hold all the love I have for this man? Maybe it all went down like this so I wouldn't lose him, so I would know that when I found him, I could run but would never need too. I guess I had to learn to count on myself so I would know how much I needed to rely on him. That if he couldn't match me, then we'd never be a match. I guess I'm not hiding anymore, and that is as equally as scary as it is lovely. Nadia smirked as she rolled her eyes and yawned, finally tired as the clock inside struck 2 am.

"Baby girl, what are you doing? How are

you still awake?" Dan asked in his sleepy voice, rubbing his eyes and blinking slowly.

"I'm just finishing off my journal entry, Daddy. I can't sleep tonight. I needed to get this out of my system. You may have been right about that," Nadia replied as he picked her up, sitting down where she had been and placing her on top of his lap, reading her laptop screen.

"Deep, bubba!" He exclaimed, kissing her shoulder and holding her close.

"Do you like it?" Nadia asked hoping that he wouldn't be mad about the stuff she wrote about marrying him. Nodding, Dan looked up at her and chuckled.

"I had just assumed that I'd be the one proposing, do you want to do it?" He asked her, playfully biting into her.

"I think so, I think I'd feel too trapped if you did it," Nadia replied, biting her bottom lip. Dan thought for a moment, before sticking out his bottom lip.

"I love that you always keep things so

interesting. I'm excited to see what ring you'll get me! I don't have such a big ego that I can't let you do it. When and if you feel like it is right," Dan said, kissing Nadia on the cheek before standing up and carrying her into their bedroom, tucking her in and holding her as she fell asleep, a smile on her lips and peace in her heart as she spoke the words which always melted his heart.

"I love you, Daddy," the last words uttered for the day, the only ones he ever needed to hear.

Who is Tina Moore?

Tina Moore has enjoyed the lifestyle of a Mommy Domme for several years. She began exploring kink and BDSM in her youth and found her love of being a strict Mommy Domme in early 2000. Tina Moore is now an author of many MDLG, DDLG and ABDL themed novels.

Follow her on:

Author Page on Amazon

Instagram @tinamoore.kdp

If you enjoyed this book, it would be much appreciated if you leave **a review on Amazon**.

www.ingramcontent.com/pod-product-compliance
Lightning Source LLC
Chambersburg PA
CBHW030704190726
48286CB00001B/164